Andy Watson

Nancy Drew
in
The Secret of Shadow Ranch

The Nancy Drew Mystery Stories

The Secret of
Shadow Ranch

Carolyn Keene

Armada

First published in the U.K. by William Collins Sons
& Co. Ltd. First published in Armada 1973 by William
Collins Sons & Co. Ltd., 14 St. James's Place, London S.W.1.

This impression 1974

Printed in Great Britain by
Love & Malcomson Ltd., Brighton Road,
Redhill, Surrey.

CONTENTS

A Curious Stranger

"HERE I am, girls!" exclaimed Nancy Drew as she hugged her two best friends. "All set for an exciting holiday at Shadow Ranch."

"I hope you had a good flight," said Bess Marvin. The pretty, slightly plump blonde was not smiling as usual. Nancy wondered why.

"Are we glad to see you!" remarked George Fayne, an attractive tomboyish girl with short dark hair. She glanced anxiously around the crowded waiting room in the Phoenix air terminal. "Let's go where we can talk."

Nancy looked at the cousins with keen blue eyes. "What's the matter? Is something wrong?"

Bess bit her lip, then burst out, "Oh, Nancy, we can't stay! We all have to go home tomorrow!"

"But why?" asked Nancy, astonished.

"Because there's a mystery at the ranch," George said bluntly, "and Uncle Ed thinks it's not safe for us to be here."

Bess put in, "But, Nancy, if you could convince Uncle Ed you can solve the case, maybe he'd let us stay. However, I'm not so sure I want to. It's—it's really pretty frightening."

"I can't wait to hear what the mystery is," Nancy said excitedly.

George insisted on collecting Nancy's suitcases at the baggage-claim section. "But save the mystery until I come back!" George said and hastened off. Bess led Nancy towards an attractive sandwich shop in the air terminal.

On the way, admiring glances were cast at the two girls. Titian-haired Nancy was a trim figure in her olive-green knitted suit with matching shoes. Beige accessories and a knitting bag completed her costume. Bess wore a pale-blue cotton dress which showed off her deep suntan to advantage.

While they walked, Bess explained that her uncle had decided at breakfast to send the girls home. At his insistence, George had made reservations for a flight the next day.

"We told him what a wonderful detective you are and begged him to let you try to solve the mystery. He said it was too dangerous for a girl. George phoned you, but you'd already left." Bess sighed. "It's a shame! We could have had a super holiday!"

The three girls had grown up together in River Heights, and had shared many exciting adventures.

Several weeks before, Bess and George's aunt and uncle, Edward and Elizabeth Rawley, owners of Shadow Ranch, had invited them to spend the summer in Arizona. The Rawleys had easily been persuaded to include Nancy in the invitation.

Nancy's father, Carson Drew, a famous lawyer, had given his consent to the trip, but had asked his daughter to delay her departure for a week in order to do some work for him.

Now the young sleuth was eager to hear about the mystery at Shadow Ranch. She and Bess strolled into the sandwich shop and made their way among the crowded tables to a small one in a corner.

As they seated themselves, a slender grey-haired man in a tan suit sat down at the next table. Nancy placed her knitting bag on the floor between his chair and her own.

"What are you making?" Bess asked, nodding towards the bag.

"A sweater for Ned," Nancy replied. "I hope to finish it for his birthday. Originally I bought the wool for myself, but he admired the colour, so I decided to surprise him and knit a sweater for him. Do you think he'll like the style?"

"He'll love it. Not to change the subject, but there are some handsome cowboys at the ranch," Bess remarked. As she told Nancy of the fun she and George had been having, Bess grew more cheerful.

Just then George joined them. Besides the brown linen handbag that matched her dress, she now carried a big vacuum flask.

"I had a porter put your bags in the car," she told Nancy, "and I brought this flask back. We have to fill it with water for the drive across the desert. We started with two flasks. Bess and I finished the water in the other one on the way here."

When the waitress came to take the girls' order, Nancy and George chose soft drinks, while Bess studied the menu.

"This mystery has me so upset," she declared, "that my appetite is gone." Then she added, "I'll have a double chocolate sundae with walnuts."

Nancy and George grinned. "Poor girl," said George, "she's wasting away."

Bess looked sheepish. "Never mind me," she said. "Start telling Nancy about the mystery."

George tugged her chair closer and bent forward. "About two months ago," she began, "Uncle Ed and Aunt Bet acquired Shadow Ranch in payment of a debt. They'd always wanted to be ranchers, so they moved there and began working the property. But for the past month there have been so many accidents that they've decided the ranch is being sabotaged."

"At first they weren't sure"—Bess took up the story—"but after last night, Uncle Ed said there was no doubt."

"What happened?" Nancy asked.

"The phantom horse appeared," replied George.

Nancy's eyes sparkled with interest. "A phantom! Tell me!"

Bess shivered. "It's the weirdest thing—all glowing white and filmy! We saw it running across what we call the big meadow."

George added, "Shorty Steele—he's one of the ranch hands—says it's supposed to be the ghost of the horse which belonged to Dirk Valentine, an old-time outlaw."

"There's a very romantic legend about him," Bess said. "He was the sweetheart of Frances Humber, daughter of the local sheriff, who was the original owner of Shadow Ranch. One night when Dirk Valentine came there to see Frances, the sheriff shot and killed him. As he lay dying, the desperado put a curse on the Humber property, vowing that his horse would haunt Shadow Ranch. And whenever it appeared, destruction would follow."

"That curse came true," George said grimly. "This morning Uncle Ed found one of his windmills had been pulled down."

Nancy looked thoughtful. "Did the phantom horse make any sound?"

"No," replied George, "but just before it appeared we heard a weird whistle. The ranchers say the outlaw always called his horse that way."

"The phantom horse must be a trick, of course," said Nancy. "It sounds as if someone is trying to scare your aunt and uncle off their property." As she spoke, Nancy became aware that the man at the next table was listening intently to the conversation.

"But why—" Bess broke off as she felt Nancy's foot nudge hers under the table. George caught Nancy's warning glance and also understood.

Just then the waitress brought their order and the girls chatted lightly of other subjects. When they finished and their bill had come, Nancy reached for her knitting bag and gave a cry of alarm.

"What's the matter?" Bess asked.

"My bag! I can't find it."

George exclaimed, "I'll bet that man who sat next to us took it! He's gone too!"

The three girls jumped up and looked around, but the man was not in sight. George hurried outside to see if she could find him.

Nancy, meanwhile, looked on the floor nearby. Under the far side of the man's table lay the knitting bag. Quickly Nancy retrieved it.

"See if anything's missing!" Bess advised. "Maybe your purse has gone!"

Nancy made a search, but as far as she could tell, the original contents were intact. However, their arrangement seemed to be different. Had the man been snooping—and if so, why?

Bess paid the bill and the girls walked to the door. They met George coming in. "Didn't see him anywhere," she said. "I suppose he drove off. The thief! He—" George stopped. "Nancy, you have your bag!"

Nancy grinned. "Thanks for your help, anyway."

"I still don't like Old Eavesdropper," George declared.

As the girls walked through the terminal, Nancy stopped at a row of telephone kiosks. "Wait a moment," she said. "I promised to call home and let Hannah know when I arrived here."

Bess volunteered to fill the vacuum flask while Nancy phoned. "Give my love to Hannah," she called back as she hurried off.

"Mine, too," said George as Nancy entered the phone box.

Mrs Hannah Gruen was the Drews' warm-hearted housekeeper who had looked after Nancy since her mother's death when she was three. She and Nancy held a deep affection for each other.

Soon Hannah's cheerful voice came over the phone. "Don't worry about anything here, Nancy," she said. "Just enjoy yourself."

By the time Nancy hung up, Bess had returned. "I didn't tell Hannah I might be straight home," Nancy reported.

"She's going to get a big surprise when we turn up tomorrow," George remarked gloomily.

Nancy smiled. "Not if I can persuade your uncle to change his mind."

As the girls stepped from the cool building the afternoon sun was dazzling. Waves of heat shimmered over the parked cars.

"What are you doing?" George called to the stranger

George led the way past several lines of cars, then turned into a row and walked towards an old estate car. As the girls drew closer, they exclaimed in surprise. A man was dropping something through the open window of the car! *He was the eavesdropper who had sat beside them!*

"What are you doing?" George called.

The stranger glanced up, startled, then darted away among the cars.

Nancy dashed to the estate car, with the girls close behind her. There was a piece of paper on the seat.

Nancy picked it up. "A note!"

In crudely pencilled letters it said: "*Keep away from Shadow Ranch.*"

"Come on!" Nancy exclaimed. "We must catch that man and find out what this means!"

· 2 ·

Dangerous Surprises

THE girls sped off in the direction in which the man had fled. At the end of the row of cars, they paused to look right and left.

"There he is!" Nancy exclaimed. The man was hastening towards the terminal. He looked back, then broke into a run.

Nancy and George sprinted ahead and saw him dash into the building. The girls followed, dodging people and luggage trucks, but the fugitive had disappeared among the crowd.

"Where is he?" Bess panted as she caught up with them.

"Gone," George said tersely. "No use looking for him in here."

But Nancy had not given up. Their dash into the terminal had excited curious stares from passers-by and a news attendant.

"Did you ever see that man before?" she asked the assistant behind the newspaper counter. "The one we were chasing?"

"No," he said. "What happened? Did he steal something? Should I call the police?"

"No, thank you," said Nancy. "But I'd like to find out who he is."

She questioned some other people nearby, but none of them had ever seen the man before.

Nancy returned to the cousins. "I'm afraid that's that." As they left the building, Nancy realized that she was still holding the note and tucked it into her knitting bag.

"One thing we've learned," she said as they crossed the car park again, "whoever the man is, he's connected with the mystery at the ranch."

"But why should he want to keep us away from there?" Bess asked.

"Perhaps for the same reason someone wants to drive your aunt and uncle off the property," Nancy replied.

When they reached the car, Nancy volunteered to drive. George agreed and acted as her guide through the streets of Phoenix.

As they left the outskirts, the road stretched before them like an endless white ribbon with brown desert on either side as far as the eye could see. Here and there were dark clumps of sage and salt grass. Beyond, on the horizon, lay the hazy blue shapes of mountains.

"That's where we're headed, pardner," George said with a grin. "One hundred and fifty miles of the hottest, thirstiest ride you ever took!"

For a while cars passed the girls from both directions, then grew fewer and fewer.

Bess, who had been unusually silent, spoke up. "What I can't work out is why anybody would want to take Shadow Ranch from Uncle Ed. It's in very poor condition."

George agreed. "It almost seems as if Dirk Valentine's curse has worked." She told Nancy that shortly after the outlaw's death, Sheriff Humber's fortunes had begun to fail. He had been forced to sell the ranch, section by section. One large part was now state property, on which old Indian cliff dwellings still stood. Finally Humber had lost the property altogether.

The next owner had tried to build it up, but he too had suffered bad luck. Others had followed and with each the ranch had fallen into a worse state of disrepair. Ed Rawley had been obliged to sink a lot of money into the place, trying to get it into running condition.

Nancy had listened thoughtfully. "The property must have some hidden value," she said, "if somebody wants it so badly now."

For a while the girls rode without speaking. The wind had risen and the rush of it past the open windows, combined with the roar of the engine, made conversation difficult.

Suddenly Bess gave a sharp exclamation. "Nancy! We completely forgot to tell you about Alice!"

George slapped her forehead. "My goodness! What brains we are!"

"Alice who?" asked Nancy.

"Our cousin, Alice Regor. She's fourteen," replied Bess. "She's staying at Shadow Ranch, too."

"That is, she hopes she's staying," George amended. "If we go home, she'll have to leave too."

"I feel sorry for her," Bess said. "She has a special reason for being here—and she's hoping you can help her, Nancy."

"Me?" Nancy exclaimed. "How?"

"We've told her about you," Bess confessed, "and what a good detective you are."

Nancy laughed. "Now, Bess, you know you don't

have to butter me up. Just tell me—what is Alice's mystery?"

Bess smiled. "I knew you'd try to help."

George explained, "Alice's father is missing. He's been gone almost six months."

She said that Ross Regor had been president of a bank in a suburb of Chicago, where he had lived with his family. Someone reported having seen him enter the bank on the night it was robbed. Mr Regor had not been seen since.

"Some of the newspapers implied that he was in league with the gang," Bess said, "but naturally none of his family or friends believes that."

"From the way the burglar alarm was tampered with," George said, "the police were able to identify the gang easily. A few days later one of them was spotted in Phoenix, but eluded capture.

"Because of that, Alice thinks the gang is hiding out in this area and holding her father captive. Or, if he was released, he's wandering around here, a victim of amnesia."

Nancy was instantly sympathetic. "That's not much to go on, but I'll do my best."

During the past five minutes the wind had been increasing and Nancy was using considerable strength to keep the wheel steady. Suddenly a brown swirling cloud of sand arose ahead of them.

"Sandstorm!" she cried. "Close the windows!"

Her words were lost as the wind shrieked and a stinging flash of sand hit their faces. While Nancy fought to hold the car on the road, Bess leaned behind her and managed to wind up the window. George closed the one on her side.

Nancy applied the brakes and the girls sat silent, astounded by the suddenness of the storm. The wind screamed and the sand sifted through the cracks round the windows and doors. The car rocked but stayed upright.

"Wow!" said George. "This desert is full of surprises!"

"Dangerous ones," Bess added.

After an agonizing wait, the wind gradually died and the sand settled enough to permit the girls to see the red glow of the sun. Quickly they opened the doors and stepped outside.

"Ugh," said Bess, shaking her head. "I have sand in my hair!"

When they had brushed their clothes, Bess took one of the flasks from the back of the car. Quickly she poured water into paper cups for all of them.

Nancy drank hers thirstily. "Umm, good old water," she said with a sigh.

"It was wonderful the way you held the car on the road," said Bess, helping herself to a second cup.

"Right," said George. "If we'd gone into the soft sand, we'd have been stranded!"

Nancy looked over the empty desert and shook her head. "How awful it must have been for the pioneers!" she said. "Imagine riding out here for days in a bumpy wagon or walking in the burning sun."

"With every drop of water precious," Bess said.

"They ran out of it, too, sometimes," George said soberly. "Uncle Ed told us that bones of pioneers and abandoned wagons have been found in many places."

"It's a ghastly thought," Bess remarked, and there was silence for a while.

Finally Nancy said, "If I read the mileage right, we

have about an hour's drive yet." She poured some water from the flask on to her clean handkerchief and wiped her face and hands. George and Bess did the same, then the girls combed their hair and put on fresh lipstick.

Bess giggled. "I don't know why we bother. There's no one out here to see us but prairie dogs and lizards!"

"Cheer up," said Nancy. "You'll soon be back among all those handsome cowboys!"

George poured the remaining water from the flask into a cup and offered it to the others. Nancy and Bess declined, so George drank it herself.

The girls got into the car and Nancy turned the key in the ignition. The engine started at once.

"You don't know how glad I am to hear that," she confessed. "I was afraid sand might have clogged the engine."

As the car rolled along, Nancy said, "I've been thinking about the mystery of Shadow Ranch. Tell me more of the windmill episode. If somebody tore it down, there'd have been a tremendous racket. Didn't the Rawleys hear it?"

"No," said George. "And the mill wasn't torn down. Uncle Ed thinks, from tyre tracks and bumper dents, that someone used the ranch truck, drove to the east meadow without lights, and backed hard into the windmill a few times. Over it went. That night there was a howling storm, so of course no one heard the noise."

Nancy frowned. "Aren't there any dogs on the ranch? Surely they'd have barked."

Bess nodded her head. "The Rawleys have a fine watchdog. There wasn't a peep out of him. Besides, the east meadow is some distance from the ranch building."

"Then," said Nancy, "the whole thing must have been an inside job. The dog knows the person or persons who did this. Have you noticed anything suspicious about the ranch hands?"

Bess and George said all the men seemed very nice. "But then," George added, "I suppose they'd be careful to avoid suspicion. Well, Nancy, you can see you have a job ahead of you."

"If Uncle Ed will let us stay," Bess said. "Say, is it my imagination or is it getting hotter in this wagon?" She mopped her forehead with a handkerchief. "Better start on the second flask of water."

As Bess turned round to reach for it, Nancy glanced at the temperature gauge. "Oh no!" she exclaimed. "We're overheating!"

Grimly she slowed down and stopped. The girls climbed out.

Bess leaned into the car and released the lock of the bonnet. Nancy and George, using handkerchiefs on the hot metal, tried to lift it. At first the bonnet stuck, then suddenly flew up.

"Look out!" warned Nancy, unscrewing the radiator cap. She jumped back, pulling George with her as steam and boiling water spouted from the radiator.

"Are you all right?" Bess cried anxiously as she hurried towards them.

"I am. How about you, George?"

"I'm okay," said George, brushing the moisture from her face and short-cropped hair. "Just what I didn't need. A hot bath."

"Good thing we didn't drink that other flask of water," said Nancy. "We'll need it for the radiator."

"There must be a leak in it," George said, looking worried. "The water'll run right through."

"It can't be too bad," Nancy reasoned. "After all, we came a long way before trouble started."

"That's right," George conceded. "We should be able to make it to the ranch." She went to the back of the car and quickly returned with the flask.

She removed the top and handed the jug to Nancy, who tilted it over the radiator. *Not a drop came out!*

·3·

Warning Rattle

"WE'RE stranded!" Bess exclaimed in dismay.

George stared at the empty flask unbelievingly. "It can't be!" said George. "Shorty Steele promised to fill it with water."

"He must have forgotten," said Bess. She peered up and down the road, but there was no vehicle in sight.

Nancy tried to sound unworried as she spoke. "We might as well get into the car and wait for the water in the radiator to cool off—or maybe somebody will come along and help us." She replaced the radiator cap.

"If we're not at the ranch for supper, Uncle Ed or someone will drive out to look for us," Bess remarked hopefully.

Time dragged by as the girls waited. Nancy tested the water twice. It was still boiling hot. They might have to wait until evening and she was not keen about the idea of driving in the desert after dark.

"It's like an oven in this car," Bess complained.

"Hotter outside," George mumbled.

Suddenly the girls spotted a speck moving towards them on the dusty road. With relief the girls watched it take shape as a pick-up truck.

"It's from the ranch!" George yelled, and dashed outside.

Bess followed, and when the truck stopped, she cried out, "Dave Gregory! You're a lifesaver! I was about to die of thirst and sunstroke!"

With a grin the tall, rangy cowboy swung down from the truck. Quickly Bess introduced him to Nancy.

Dave's handsome face grew stern when Bess and George explained what had happened. He pushed his hat to the back of his head, hooked his thumbs in his belt, and said, "Just what I figured. Three little dudes stuck high and dry. Mr Rawley warned you to check your water supply before you went out in the desert!"

"But Shorty promised he'd take care of it," said George.

Dave's eyes narrowed for an instant, then he said casually, "Well, this is dangerous country—you check your *own* gear, if you know what's good for you."

"We're sorry you had to come out after us," Nancy apologized.

"Mr Rawley's orders," he said coolly, and strode to the truck.

In a minute Dave was back with a large can and a vacuum flask which he handed to the girls. While they drank gratefully, he poured water from the can into the radiator of the estate car. He put back the cap and slammed down the bonnet. The girls returned the flask and thanked him.

Dave gave a curt nod, walked to his truck, and swung aboard. By the time Nancy had the car started, the pick-up had turned around and gone roaring down the road ahead of them.

"What's eating him?" George burst out. "He was about as friendly to you, Nancy, as a prairie dog!"

Nancy smiled. "Never mind. I can see his point."

She wondered, however, what the trouble was. She had not even reached the ranch and already two people had been mysterious and unfriendly to her!

She followed the truck down the highway, and finally on to a road which wound through the barren foothills of the mountains. It was nearly sunset when the girls entered a rocky pass and came out high above a valley. At the far side loomed a huge mountain with a group of low buildings nestling at its foot.

Bess pointed to them. "There's the ranch, and that's Shadow Mountain."

"I see how they got their names," said Nancy. "The great peak throws its shadow over the whole valley."

Half an hour later, they drove through a weather-beaten wooden gate into the ranch yard. Nancy pulled up to the ranch house, a long, one-storey adobe building with a vine-covered veranda across the front.

To the north of the house were the corral and stable. Beyond these stretched a large meadow, bordered by a wire fence. In the opposite direction lay the bunkhouse, and south of this, some distance away, a smaller, enclosed meadow. In it cattle were grazing.

A stocky sunburned man and a slender dark-haired woman hurried out to greet the girls as they alighted. "Bess, George!" exclaimed Elizabeth Rawley. "We were so worried. And this must be Nancy! We're very glad to see you, dear." She gave her guest a hug and a smile, but the girl could see a strained look in her eyes.

Mr Rawley took Nancy's hand in his large one and said cordially, "I'm mighty glad to know you."

"And I'm glad to be here," Nancy replied. Her host gathered the suitcases and led the way towards the house.

Suddenly Nancy heard ferocious barking and turned to see a huge black dog bounding towards her. Behind him ran Dave Gregory.

"Chief!" he shouted. "Come back here!"

With a snarl the dog stopped short and began circling Nancy, snapping and barking. She did not move and the animal grew calmer. Then, as she spoke to him softly, he sniffed her hand. Moments later, Nancy was stroking his thick fur. He was a handsome black German shepherd dog, the largest Nancy had ever seen.

The others had been looking on in amazement. "Young lady," said Ed Rawley, "I like the way you stood your ground. How about it, Dave?"

"Pretty good for a tenderfoot," the cowboy admitted, then said, "Come along, Chief. Your job is chasing coyotes away from the chickens." Obediently the dog trotted away towards the far end of the yard.

"The dog's full name is Apache Chief," said Elizabeth Rawley as she led the girls on to the veranda.

Just then a slender girl with dark curly hair and big sad-looking eyes stepped from the house. Bess introduced her as their cousin Alice. She said hello to Nancy and shyly followed the others along the veranda to Bess and George's room, which Nancy was to share. Another door led into the main hallway of the house.

Mr Rawley followed with the luggage. When the travellers had had a shower and put on fresh dresses, they heard a loud clanging from outside.

"That's cook ringing for supper," Alice explained to Nancy.

The girls hurried off to the kitchen at the far end of the house. Outside the screen door hung an iron triangle, still swinging. The big room was crowded with men who stood round a long oval table with a red-check tablecloth on it.

Nancy was introduced to a tall, thin man with sun-bleached hair. "This is Walt Sanders, my foreman," said Mr Rawley, "and some of my men."

Sanders shook Nancy's hand. Shorty Steele, a husky middle-aged cowboy, did the same. Next a good-looking red-haired cowboy was introduced as Tex Britten and his dark-haired pal as Bud Moore. With a glance Bess informed Nancy that these two were the nice cowboys she had told her about.

"Grub's ready!" called a high, shrill voice. "Every-body sit down!" A small woman with frizzy grey hair and a white apron bustled from the stove to the table bearing a big platter of steaming meat.

"This is Mrs Thurmond, our cook," said the ranch owner's wife.

In the confusion of taking seats, George had a chance to ask Shorty about the water he had promised to put in the station wagon. The cowboy's suntanned face showed surprise. "No, ma'am, I never said I'd do that," he declared. "You musta mistook my meanin'." He repeated the denial several times.

Nancy overheard Shorty and thought he was over-doing it. She wondered if "the misunderstanding" might not have been part of a plan to scare the girls away from the ranch.

After serving a hearty meal of roast beef, beans, corn fritters and salad, Mrs Thurmond produced two large delicious apple pies. When the last bite had been eaten, Ed Rawley stood up and a hush fell on the chatter at the table.

"Okay, men," he said brusquely, "who has first watch?"

"Me and Dave," replied Shorty, and the two left the kitchen together.

Quietly the rest of the men rose to leave and Mrs Rawley led the girls through a door into a large living room. Like the kitchen, it ran from the front to the back of the house.

Among the comfortable furnishings were several slim, old-fashioned rocking chairs and a round centre table with a brass lamp on it. Bright-coloured Indian rugs lay on the floor. At one end of the room was a huge stone fireplace.

"Tradition says that all the rocks in it have come from Shadow Ranch," Alice told Nancy. She pointed out a smooth round one. "That's an Indian grinding stone."

At the opposite end of the room, beside a door leading to the veranda, was a deep window. In front of it on shelves stood rows of coloured antique bottles.

"This is a lovely place!" Nancy exclaimed.

"We're sorry you can't stay to enjoy it," said Mrs Rawley as her husband entered from the kitchen.

"Yes," he added, "but it's too dangerous. We're under attack. We can't figure out by whom or why. I only know that if the damage keeps on, we won't be able to stand the expense. We'll lose Shadow Ranch."

Mrs Rawley explained that the sheriff could not spare a man to be a full-time guard at the ranch, so her husband and the hands took turns standing watch.

"Perhaps you have enemies who want revenge on you," Nancy suggested. "Or maybe your property has hidden value."

The owner replied that he could think of nothing to support either theory. Nancy then described the man at the airport and told of what had happened.

"The note's in your knitting bag," Bess spoke up. "I'll get it!"

She hurried to the girls' room and returned with Nancy's knitting bag.

The young sleuth took out the note and crossed the room to give it to the rancher. Bess started to close the bag. Instead, she idly picked up the half-finished sweater. Underneath it lay a small object loosely wrapped in dirty brown paper.

"What's this, Nancy?" she asked. As she lifted it, the wrapping fell off. For a moment Bess stared at the thing in her hand, then gave a little cry and flung it from her.

Nancy hurried to pick up the object. "The rattle from a snake," she said, holding it up for the others to see.

"Ugh!" exclaimed Alice.

Nancy retrieved the wrapping paper. There was pencilled writing on it. " 'Second warning!' " she read aloud.

Nancy turned to the grim-faced ranch owner and his wife. "Now more than ever," she said earnestly, "I want to solve this mystery. Won't you let me stay and help you?"

The rancher looked at her pleading expression and smiled. "We could certainly use a detective. And I've got to hand it to you, Nancy—you sure can keep your head." He glanced at his wife. "What do you say, Bet?"

Elizabeth Rawley nodded soberly. "All right. The girls may stay, but they must promise to be very careful."

Eagerly they agreed and George hastened to the telephone in the hall to cancel the plane reservations which she had made. In the meantime, Mr Rawley said he thought the notes and the snake rattle should be taken to the sheriff the next morning. "I'll go, Mr Rawley," said Nancy. "Maybe I should meet him."

When George returned, Mrs Rawley was saying, "Nancy, I think you should call us Aunt Bet and Uncle Ed. After all, you'll be one of our family."

Nancy grinned. "I'd love that, Aunt Bet."

"I wish you were going to work on my mystery, too," Alice said wistfully.

Nancy took the young girl's hand. "Of course I will," she said kindly, and Alice's blue eyes lit up.

Nancy told the Rawleys that she would like to get started with her sleuthing immediately. "May I question your men about the phantom horse?"

"Yes, indeed," Ed Rawley agreed.

One after another the ranch hands were summoned, but none of them could add anything to the information Bess and George had given Nancy.

"All of these men are new here," Mr Rawley told her after they had gone. "But Walt Sanders, Tex, and Bud are from an outfit in the next county. Dave's from Montana. Shorty's a drifter."

After a little more talk, Bess stifled a yawn, then suggested that the girls go to bed. She led the way out of a side door and down a hall to their room. Alice went into the next one.

Before long Bess and George were asleep, but Nancy lay wide-eyed, wondering about Dave Gregory. Why was he so hostile to her? Could he be one of the saboteurs? And what about Shorty? Was he to be trusted? Finally Nancy fell asleep.

Just after midnight she awoke suddenly, startled by a noise on the veranda. She sensed someone pausing at the door to listen. Then stealthy footsteps moved on.

"Now what was that all about?" Nancy asked herself.

Quickly she got up, put on her dressing-gown and slippers, and cautiously opened the screen door.

No one was nearby, but at the far end of the veranda, she saw a dark figure slip into the kitchen.

"Why would anyone be going in there from outdoors at this time of night?" Nancy asked herself. "I'd better find out."

She wondered if she should waken the other girls but decided against this, and tiptoed along the veranda to the kitchen. She opened the door and stepped inside the darkened room.

The next instant an unearthly shriek split the air and someone seized her!

·4·

A Red Clue

NANCY jerked one arm free from her attacker and fumbled for a light switch. Her fingers found it and the ceiling light over the dining table went on.

Clinging to her was Mrs Thurmond, the cook! She wore an old-fashioned nightgown, and her head bristled with curlers. She let go of Nancy like a hot branding iron.

"You!" she exclaimed.

"Yes me," Nancy replied, suppressing a smile. "I'm as surprised as you are, Mrs Thurmond."

"What's the matter?" demanded Ed Rawley as he and his wife, wearing dressing-gowns and slippers, hurried in from the living room.

Then Bess and George ran in from the veranda, with Alice behind them. "Nancy! You all right?"

Soon Walt Sanders, in night clothes, rushed into the kitchen. A moment later Tex and Bud clumped in. Nancy wondered where Dave and Shorty were.

"Bud and I were on watch," said the red-haired cowboy, "and were checkin' the stable when we heard the ruckus. What's up?"

Mrs Thurmond told her story. She had been asleep in her room, a small extension off the kitchen, when she had been awakened by someone coming into the kitchen through the screen door.

"I sleep light," she explained. "First I was afraid to move. I listened hard, but I didn't hear anything more, so I decided to get up and take a look. Just as I stepped out of my room, what do I see but the screen door opening and a dark figure steps in! So I jumped him and hollered."

Nancy smiled. "And I was 'him'." Then she added, "There *was* an intruder here, Mrs Thurmond, because I saw him come in."

"He must have gone into the living room, then," said Mrs Rawley. "There's no other way out."

Mrs Thurmond shook her head. "No, ma'am," she said forcefully. "That door to the living room squeaks and I didn't hear a sound."

George moved the door and the hinges made a noise. "Then where did the intruder go?" Bess asked shakily.

Nancy's keen eyes had spotted a trap door beside the old-fashioned stove. "Perhaps down there."

"If he did," Ed Rawley said grimly, "he's caught. That's the cellar and this is the only way out. Dave," he ordered, looking beyond Nancy, "come with me."

From behind her stepped the tall cowboy. He was fully dressed and carrying a torch. She turned and saw Shorty Steele standing just inside the screen door. He, too, was in his working clothes. When had they arrived? And why hadn't they gone to bed after coming off patrol duty?

As Ed Rawley lifted up the trap door, Nancy said, "I'd like to go, too, Uncle Ed."

The man hesitated, then said, "All right, but you stay well behind us."

The cowboy turned on his torch and Nancy followed the men down a flight of wooden stairs. She found herself in a shallow cellar which was empty except for a row of shelves against one wall.

At Nancy's request Dave held his light downwards so that she could look for footprints. But the earth floor was hard-packed and she could see no marks on it.

When the trio returned to the kitchen and reported no sign of the intruder, the cook shook her head. "He was a phantom," she declared, "just like that horse."

"Now, Mrs Thurmond," said Aunt Bet, "maybe you were so excited you didn't hear the intruder go through the living-room door."

The little woman looked indignant. "I have excellent hearing," she stated, "and that door *positively* did not squeak." Nancy found it hard to doubt Mrs Thurmond's word.

The young sleuth turned to Dave. "Did you just come from the bunkhouse?"

"No," Dave said quietly. "I was doing some extra investigating."

"Whatever that means," Nancy thought. She noted that Shorty had said nothing.

Mr Rawley did not question the men. A few minutes later everyone went back to bed except Tex and Bud.

Nancy woke at dawn and puzzled over the problem. Who was the intruder? What was he after? Where had he gone? Quietly she rose and dressed, then went to the kitchen to make herself a cup of tea.

Not wanting to heat the big kettle of water which stood on the old-fashioned range, she took a small pot from a hook on the wall and carried it to the sink. She turned one of the taps but no water came out. Surprised, Nancy tried the other, with the same result. "That's strange. I'll ask the girls about it."

She hurried to the bedroom and woke them. Bess and George said this had not happened before and George went to tell her aunt and uncle.

In a short time the hastily-dressed rancher appeared, completely puzzled. He led the way past the stable and the corral to a small wooden shed. Inside were an electric generator and pump.

After examining the machinery, Ed Rawley said one grim word, "Sabotage!" He showed the girls where some of the bearings were missing. "We'll need new ones before we can have any water."

"It's a shame!" George declared. "When do you think this mischief was done? And where were the guards?"

"What difference does it make?" her uncle said with a sigh. "The men can't be everywhere at once."

"What about Chief?" Nancy asked. "He didn't bark at the saboteur. Does this mean he knows him?"

Ed Rawley's jaw tightened. "I'd trust Sanders, Bud, and Dave with my life. They came highly recommended by friends of mine. As for the others, I accuse no man without proof."

"Nor would I," Nancy said quietly, and began looking for evidence. On the wooden floor were damp daubs of red earth. Outside the building was a wet patch of the same colour, but the prints were too confused to be distinguishable.

"Whoever damaged the pump may still have this kind of mud on his boots," Nancy thought.

The rancher's face was grey with worry. "This pump will have to be fixed as soon as possible. After the windmill in the east meadow was wrecked, I had to start using this pump, which only supplied the house, to water my cattle. There's another mill in the big meadow, but its supply is not enough for them. We're lucky to have one other source of spring water."

The three girls volunteered to carry water to the kitchen. They went to get buckets from Mrs Thurmond, who was pale and tight-lipped. She handed them kettles and large pots. Bess led the way round the house to the spring house, a windowless adobe structure built on to the back wall of the kitchen.

George opened the heavy wooden door and the girls stepped down on to an earthen floor. It was cool and so dim they could barely see the small stream of water coming from a pipe in the centre.

While waiting her turn to fill her kettle, Nancy went outside to look round. Between the ranch house and the foot of Shadow Mountain she noticed that a thickly wooded strip of land ran down to abut the big meadow.

"That's where the phantom horse is supposed to appear," Nancy reflected.

Just then Bess came from the spring house. "Your turn, Nancy," she called.

The young sleuth hurried inside and placed her kettle under the stream of water. While waiting for it to fill she noticed a stone vat against the kitchen wall. It was about three feet square with a hinged wooden lid. "That's where the old-timers stored milk products and eggs," she thought.

When Nancy reached the kitchen with her full kettle, Mrs Thurmond was serving breakfast. As the girls sat down, Dave and Shorty came in. Nancy glanced at their boots. There was damp red mud on both pairs!

As soon as the men had finished eating, Dave stood up. "I'm going to Tumbleweed to get pump bearings," he said to Nancy. "Mr Rawley said you wanted to do an errand in town. You can ride along with me."

Nancy was glad the sheriff had not been mentioned. She said, "I'll go, thank you, and I'll bring George."

Dave scowled. "I'll be in the pick-up," he replied abruptly and walked out.

Nancy hurried to her room to get the warning notes and the rattle. The pick-up was parked in the yard, and as soon as Nancy and George had climbed into the cab, Dave started it.

Without saying a word, he drove out of the ranch gate and turned on to a track which stretched down the valley. The girls appeared to be relaxed, but they could not rid their minds of a distrust of Dave.

Once he caught Nancy looking at his shoes. "Yes, Miss Detective," he said, "that's mud from outside the pump house. I was up before dawn this morning, and thought I heard a noise there. I didn't find anyone, though. Must have scared off the pump-wrecker, but he came back later."

George asked why Dave was up so early, but he did not answer or speak again until they reached a small town of old-fashioned wooden buildings. The cowboy parked the pick-up on the main street.

"I'll meet you here in half an hour," he said as he swung out of the truck. Nancy and George saw him go into a hardware shop several doors away. In front of the girls was a building with a sign: SHERIFF.

As the girls entered the small office a grey-haired man swivelled round in his chair and rose to greet them. "I reckon you're Miss Drew," he said in a pleasant drawl. "I'm Sheriff Curtis." His eyes twinkled. "Ed Rawley told me you're aimin' to help him find what's causin' the trouble at the ranch."

George spoke up. "And she will, if she can."

"I sure wish you luck."

After hearing Nancy's story and looking at the notes and rattle, he said, "I'll hang on to these as evidence and phone the state and Phoenix lawmen to keep an eye out for the hombre you saw at the airport. Keep me posted," he added gravely, "and be extra careful, girls."

Nancy thanked him and the callers left. They still had twenty minutes to spare. George said she wanted to purchase a cowboy kerchief in the general store, so Nancy strolled along looking in shop-windows. The town seemed almost deserted and many of the shops were not yet open.

Ahead, in the centre of the street, grew a large cottonwood tree with a wooden bench built round the trunk. Nancy walked to it and was about to sit in the shade, when her eye was caught by a tall stack of Indian baskets outside a shop marked: MARY DEER— GIFTS.

Nancy crossed over to look at them, then glanced through the window. Startled at what she saw, Nancy almost cried out. The shop was empty, except for a man with a black kerchief covering his face to the eyes. He was crouching in front of an open glass case, scooping jewellery into a paper bag!

Heart pounding, Nancy looked up and down the

street for help. But there was no one in sight. Boldly she stepped to the open door of the shop.

"Drop that bag!" she ordered.

With a startled gasp the man whirled, then charged straight at her.

· 5 ·

Desperado's Gift

THINKING quickly, Nancy jumped aside and toppled the tower of baskets into the thief's path. With a cry he stumbled among them and pitched forward, the bag of loot flying from his hand.

"Help!" shouted Nancy as she ran into the street and picked up the paper bag. "Sheriff!"

The man scrambled to his feet, and kicking the baskets aside, darted into a narrow passage between two shops.

At the same time, a young Indian girl and a man ran from the coffee shop next door.

"What happened?" cried the girl. "I'm Mary Deer." Quickly Nancy told her about the thief. "My shop— robbed!" she exclaimed.

"Almost robbed," said Nancy, smiling and handing over the brown paper bag. As the girl thanked her warmly, George, Dave, Sheriff Curtis, and a few merchants ran up. Nancy repeated her story rapidly and described the thief. "He wore a black kerchief over his nose and mouth, was in shirt sleeves, and had on dark trousers."

As the men dashed into the passage where he had vanished, Nancy turned to the Indian girl. She was wearing a vivid red beaded dress and had a glossy black braid over each shoulder. Nancy introduced herself and George.

Gratefully Mary Deer said, "You were wonderful to get this back for me, Nancy. I would like to give you a reward."

"That's not necessary. I'm glad I could help."

Mary Deer invited the girls into the shop, which was cool and smelled of leather goods. To one side stood a long glass case containing shelves of jewellery. One front panel was open and a shelf was empty.

"There's no lock on the case," Mary explained. "I guess I shouldn't have left the shop open, but I never expected customers so early." Then she added, "Where are you from? You don't sound like a Westerner."

Nancy explained that she was a visitor at Shadow Ranch.

The Indian girl smiled. "Then I have the perfect reward for you." She reached into the paper bag and took out a small gold object. It was a lady's old-fashioned watch on a fleur-de-lis pin.

"How beautiful!" Nancy exclaimed. "But I can't accept it. Surely you can sell the watch."

Mary Deer shook her head. "This is not for sale. I had it on display in my antique jewellery case. Since you are from Shadow Ranch, it shall be yours."

"But what has the ranch to do with it?" Nancy asked curiously.

The Indian girl explained that the watch had been a gift to Frances Humber from her outlaw sweetheart. "Here is his initial," she said, and pointed to a "V" and the date, June, 1880, inscribed on the back lid. Then she turned the watch over and showed Nancy a heart inscribed on the front. "That was Valentine's symbol," said Mary Deer. "Legend says he used it on personal belongings like his belt buckle and rings—even the brand on his horse was a heart."

"He sounds like a romantic man," remarked Nancy.

Mary agreed. "He left Frances a treasure," she went on, "but she never received it."

"A treasure?" Nancy said. "What was it?"

Mary shrugged. "Valentine's will merely stated that his personal fortune was to go to Frances and her heirs. The will did not tell where or what the treasure was. Some believe it was hidden on Shadow Ranch."

Nancy's heart leaped with excitement. Maybe this could explain the sabotage at the ranch! "Someone wants to force the Rawleys off the property in order to search for the treasure," she thought.

"Do many people know about this?" George asked.

"Nearly everybody round here has heard Valentine's story, except the part about the treasure being hidden on the ranch, which is something that only a few old-timers believed." Mary shook her head. "I doubt whether the present owners of Shadow Ranch have ever heard about it."

Carefully Nancy examined the gold watch. Perhaps there was a clue to the treasure in it! She pressed her nail against the edge and opened the lid, revealing the worn face of the watch.

"It still works," said Mary. "The back lid opens, too."

Nancy was disappointed to find that there was no picture or inscription inside either place.

"Where did you get the watch?" she asked.

"It was in a box of things I bought at an auction," the Indian girl replied. She explained that the items had belonged to an old resident of Tumbleweed, Miss Melody Phillips, who had been a girlhood friend of Frances Humber. "Frances died in the East, and her parents, who still lived on the ranch, gave these mementos to Miss Melody. I know this history because it was written on the cover of the box."

"Do you still have that?" Nancy asked eagerly.

The Indian girl shook her head regretfully. "I threw the box and the other items away since they were worthless. You must take the watch, Nancy," she added earnestly. "Please."

Not wanting to hurt the girl's feelings, Nancy consented. As she was thanking her, Dave strode into the shop. He reported that the thief had not been caught. "Sheriff says he'll keep an eye out for him, Mary."

"That's good," the young shop owner said, then showed Dave the watch. "I'm giving this to Nancy," she added, and repeated the history of the timepiece.

Dave seemed to be interested and examined the watch closely. When he returned it, Mary pinned it shyly to Nancy's blouse.

As the girls were leaving the shop with Dave, Nancy noticed a small pastel drawing propped up on the counter. "What a beautiful scene!" she remarked.

Mary said it was the work of an artist who lived on Shadow Mountain. Struck by the lovely Western landscape, Nancy bought the picture.

When the group walked outside, Nancy saw a tall man in black jacket and pants seated on the bench under the cottonwood tree. He wore a black ten-gallon hat, and his light-brown eyes followed Nancy as she passed him. It seemed to her that his gaze was

"Come and rope me, pardner!" Bud challenged Bess

fastened on the watch. Could he be the frustrated thief?

"He might have left his coat and hat somewhere," Nancy reasoned, "and put them on again after his escape. But why should he be interested in the watch, unless he's after the Humber treasure and hoped to find a clue in it?"

As Dave drove out of town, Nancy saw the tall stranger staring after them. "The name of the ranch is on the side of the truck," she thought uneasily. "If that man *is* after this watch, he'll know just where to find me!"

Halfway to the ranch, the girls pointed out Indian cliff dwellings high on the mountain slope. Nancy asked if this was the area once owned by the Humbers and Dave nodded.

"Good place to look for curios like pieces of pottery," George remarked.

"You girls stay away from there!" he advised sharply. When Nancy asked why, Dave explained that the stairs leading up from the valley floor were worn and broken. "Very dangerous," he said.

When they reached the ranch, Dave parked the truck at the stable. The girls heard laughter coming from the corral and saw Tex Britten perched on the fence. Bess was mounted on a brown horse and holding a coiled lariat.

"Watch me!" she called. "I'm learning to rope a steer."

Nancy and George walked over and saw Bud Moore put his hands on his head like horns and prance in front of Bess's horse. "Come on and rope me, pardner!" he said.

Bess frowned, bit her lip, and managed to get a noose twirling. Then *plop*—it dropped over the head of her own horse!

Tex gave a piercing whistle. George and Nancy burst into laughter while the "steer" helped blushing Bess to dismount.

"Never mind," said Nancy. "You didn't want to be a cowboy, anyway!"

As the boys called joking remarks about the next roping lesson, the girls walked off together. At the house Nancy told Bess, Aunt Bet, and Alice all that had happened in town. She showed them the watch and related its history.

"Shorty Steele is the one who told us the legend of the phantom horse," said Aunt Bet, "but he never mentioned the treasure. Maybe he doesn't know that part of the story."

"Or perhaps he kept it to himself," Nancy thought. Aloud she said, "Would it be all right if we hunt for the treasure?"

"By all means."

While the others were examining the old-fashioned watch, Nancy took the pastel picture from her bag and propped it on the living-room table.

Alice saw it and turned pale. "Nancy! Where did you get this?"

As Nancy explained, Alice picked up the painting. "My father did this—I'm sure of it!" She told them that Ross Regor was an amateur artist and always carried a small case of pastels with him. Whenever he had a few leisure minutes he devoted the time to sketching and Alice was positive she could recognize his work.

"We must find the artist," she said. "I just know he's my father!"

The others could not help feeling that Alice was clutching at straws. Nevertheless, Aunt Bet offered to take her young niece to town the next morning to question Mary Deer.

That night after supper Nancy slipped into a heavy jacket, took a torch, and went for a walk alone. She made her way past the stable, chicken coops and corral to the edge of the big meadow. As she stood thinking, the wind whistled down the valley and tossed the treetops. Chief came padding over from the stable and nuzzled her hand.

Nancy turned and looked back. There was a light shining through a crack in the spring-house wall! "Who'd be there now?" she wondered.

As she hurried to investigate, one foot stepped on a large twig. *Crack!* In a moment the light went out!

Her sleuthing instincts aroused, Nancy tiptoed to the door, pulled it open, and shone her light inside. Empty!

A shiver ran up Nancy's spine. It was impossible!

She walked away slowly, puzzling over the incident. Suddenly a long weird whistle sounded in the direction of the meadow. From among the bordering trees—as if in response to the whistle—galloped a white, filmy horse! The phantom!

· 6 ·

Shorty's Shortcut

FOR a moment Nancy froze at the sight of the ghostly steed galloping across the meadow. Then she raced towards the fence, calling the alarm.

At the same time a yell came from the stable. "Phantom—phantom!" It was Shorty's voice. "Saddle up, everybody!"

There were answering shouts as the cowboys appeared on the run and dashed to the stable. The other girls rushed up to Nancy who was staring over the fence into the meadow. Chief joined the excited group. He began barking and made a beeline for the phantom horse, which had turned and seemed to be floating towards the far end of the meadow.

Soon the mounted ranchmen thundered out of the stable. Shorty took the lead. "Come on! This time we're gonna run that critter to earth!"

But the phantom horse was already far ahead of the pursuers. Only the dog was getting close. As the girls watched, the eerie figure reached the line of trees at the far end of the meadow. In the wink of an eye it vanished.

Bess drew a shuddering breath. "The ghost's gone! Right into thin air!"

"Nonsense," George said gruffly.

"How can anything disappear like that?" asked Alice.

"It's amazing," Nancy admitted. "We should have been able to see it glowing among the trees for a few moments." Suddenly she remembered the prophecy that destruction would follow any appearance of the phantom. "Come on!" she exclaimed. "The real trouble is somewhere else."

She and the other girls hurried back to the house. All seemed quiet there. A glance into the kitchen showed Aunt Bet trying to calm Mrs Thurmond. The girls hastened on to their rooms.

With an exclamation of dismay Nancy stopped in the doorway. The room she shared with the cousins was a shambles! Pillows were ripped, blankets lay on the floor. All the drawers had been dumped. Alice ran next door to her room and came back to say that it had not been touched.

"Someone wants us to leave Shadow Ranch, all right," George declared.

"More than that," Nancy said thoughtfully. "Someone may be looking for Frances Humber's watch."

"But only we girls and the Rawleys know Mary Deer gave it to Nancy," Alice objected.

"You're forgetting the man in town," Nancy said, "and Dave. Both were very much interested in it."

"Well, where *is* the watch?" asked Bess, looking fearful.

"I'm wearing it," said Nancy, "under my sweater." Before supper she had changed to a yellow blouse and skirt with a matching pullover.

While she and Bess and George began to clear up the mess, Alice hurried to the kitchen to tell her aunt and Mrs Thurmond what had happened. They hurried back to help. By the time the beds were made again and the pillows replaced with spare ones, the men had returned.

"The phantom got away," Ed Rawley said gloomily. "Chief was at his heels, but he hasn't come back and it worries me."

"I'm sorry," said Nancy. "I'm afraid we have other bad news for you." Quickly she reported what had happened.

"The purpose of the phantom is clear," she declared. "It's to frighten you and attract attention to the meadow while the real damage is being done somewhere else."

"If we could only catch the thing, it would surely give us a clue to who is doing all this," Ed Rawley said, and Nancy agreed.

The next morning at breakfast Dave reported that Chief still had not returned.

"The phantom got him, poor dog," Mrs Thurmond said dolefully. "Same as it will get us all."

As soon as the meal was over, Nancy said she was going out for a ride. She put on riding clothes and hastened to the stable where Tex saddled a handsome bay for her. Nancy was a skilful rider and she enjoyed the gallop in the meadow looking for clues to the phantom. But whatever marks it had left had been obscured by the pursuing horsemen.

At the far end of the field, Nancy rode into the copse of cottonwood trees where the strange creature had vanished. Here she found a path which led to the foot of the mountain and up the slope. Had the phantom gone that way?

Nancy reined her horse about and hurried to the ranch house, where she rounded up Bess and George. "Want to join me in a search party?"

"You bet," her friends chorused.

Shorty offered to lead them and within half an hour the four riders were following the path up the mountain.

It was a steep, high climb. All was silent, except for the creak of the saddles and the clop of the horses' hoofs on the stones. Finally the path levelled off and they came to a narrow stream, which they splashed across.

"This is just a small stream now," said Shorty. "But come one good cloudburst—and it'll turn into a roarin' flood so bad only a river horse could cross it. That's the kind you're ridin' now. They're big and don't get rattled—know how to swim with the current."

Near noon Nancy suddenly reined up. "Listen!" she said. Somewhere among the rocks overhead a dog was barking. Apache Chief?

Within a moment George glimpsed the roof of a cabin among the crags above. "Maybe Chief's up there!" she exclaimed.

Nancy observed that it looked as though the path they were on would lead to the cabin.

"I know a shortcut. Come with me," Shorty said quickly.

He rode ahead and led them to a side path. He explained to the girls that the other route became impassable farther up the mountain. After they had ridden for fifteen minutes Shorty stopped, pulled off his hat, and wiped his forehead with his bandanna.

"I gotta confess we strayed on to the wrong trail." He shrugged. "No use goin' back up. Gettin' too late. We better make tracks for the ranch."

Disappointed, Nancy and her friends followed him along a new trail which eventually rejoined the first path. They reached Shadow Ranch in mid-afternoon.

When they dismounted in front of the stable, Shorty said, "I'm mighty sorry we didn't find that dog."

Nancy replied, "So am I." She could not help suspecting that Shorty had pretended to be lost and deliberately kept them away from the cabin. She made up her mind to go back. The three girls discussed the possibility of his having double-crossed them.

"I'll bet he did!" George declared.

At the house they found Alice waiting for them, her face glowing. "Nancy," she cried out, "Mary Deer says the artist's name is Bursey and he lives in a cabin on Shadow Mountain!" The older girls exchanged meaningful looks.

"Alice," Nancy said happily, "I think I know where it is. We'll go there tomorrow. Maybe we'll find Chief, too."

That night Alice came to the girls' room. She was puzzled. If the artist *was* her father, why was Chief with him?

"I wish I could answer," said Nancy. "And, Alice dear, please don't get your hopes up too high. It may not be the cabin where the artist lives, although I have a hunch it's connected with the mystery of Shadow Ranch."

As Nancy spoke, she was turning the old-fashioned watch over in her hand. Absently she ran her finger along the front edge and suddenly felt a tiny obstruction. She pushed it and instantly a thin lid sprang forward.

"Why—it's a secret compartment!" she exclaimed.

On the top side of the lid was the small faded photograph of a handsome man with flowing dark hair.

"That must be Dirk Valentine!" Nancy cried, and showed it to the other girls. In the frame next to the picture of the man was a tiny corner from another picture.

"That one's been torn out," said Alice.

"It must have been a photo of Frances Humber," Bess observed.

Carefully Nancy removed the old picture. On the back in faded ink was the initial "V". In tiny script under it were the words: "*green bottle in—*"

"In *where*?" asked George.

"Perhaps the place is named on the back of the missing photograph," Nancy suggested.

"Let me see it," Bess requested.

Nancy handed her the watch. Bess looked it over carefully. Finally she sighed, replaced the picture, and put the timepiece on the dresser. "What can that odd message mean? If—"

At that moment the girls heard a dog whining. It came from somewhere in the darkness beyond the veranda.

Alice jumped up. "Listen!" she exclaimed. "Maybe that's Chief!"

·7·

Rockslide

THE girls dashed on to the veranda but could not see the big German shepherd dog.

"Here, Chief!" Nancy called.

From the dark yard came an answering whine, but the dog did not appear.

"Maybe he's hurt," said Bess as they walked towards the sound. Whines and barks filled the air as the searchers called again and again, but each time the sounds seemed farther away and definitely were coming from the big meadow. The girls reached the fence. Though they called repeatedly, there was only silence.

"Why wouldn't Chief come to us?" Alice asked.

The same question had been troubling Nancy, and the answer flashed into her mind. "Perhaps there wasn't any dog! Maybe someone imitated him to get us out of our room."

Bess gave a gasp of alarm. "Nancy! Your watch! I left it on the dresser!"

Hoping they would not be too late, the girls ran back to their room. All sighed in relief. The watch was still on the dresser!

"Thank goodness!" said Bess. "If it had disappeared I never would have forgiven myself."

George said, "We were gone long enough for someone to lift out Valentine's picture and look at the writing on it."

Nancy examined the picture carefully, but could detect no sign of its having been removed.

Alice spoke up. "What do you think those words on the back of the photograph mean, Nancy?"

The young detective thought they might be a clue to the treasure. "Valentine may have given the watch to Frances for a double purpose—as a gift and a way to tell her secretly where his treasure was hidden."

"You mean it's in a green bottle?" Bess asked incredulously.

Nancy shook her head. "More likely the bottle contains directions to it. Let's look over Aunt Bet's bottle collection."

She pinned the watch on to her blouse and hurried to the living room with the others. Nancy showed Mrs Rawley the clue in the secret compartment, and asked if any of the bottles in her collection had been found on the premises.

"Two," said the woman. "And one of them is green!"

The girls went to the window with her and she removed a dark-green, narrow-necked bottle from the top shelf.

"It was for liniment," she said, handing it to Nancy. "The old Western miners and ranchers used a lot of it. Collectors are always looking for those antique bottles. I found this one in an old shed behind the stable."

Nancy removed the stopper, turned the bottle over, and shook it, but nothing fell out. Nancy asked Alice to bring a knitting needle from her bag. When she returned, the girl detective probed into the bottle with the long needle.

"It's empty," was her verdict.

"We'll have to start searching the ranch for other bottles," said Bess.

That night Nancy went to sleep wondering if someone else might also be looking for the green bottle. The answer came after breakfast next morning as she crossed the living room. The green liniment bottle was gone from the window shelf!

Nancy searched the other shelves at once, but in vain. It was obvious that the dog whining had been a trick and someone had read the clue on the back of Valentine's picture!

Just then Dave passed the veranda door. Nancy called him in and asked what time he had taken guard duty the night before.

"Eight o'clock to midnight," he replied. "Why?"

"Just wondering. Did you hear a dog whine in the yard or see anyone?"

Dave had heard the dog but seen no one. When he had reached the yard, there had been no sign of the animal.

"Again, why?" The cowboy regarded Nancy quizzically.

"It was a trick to get us outside so someone could snoop in my room," Nancy replied. She looked him straight in the eye, and he met her gaze without flinching.

"I think you're right," he said, and added quietly, "Be careful, Nancy. You're on dangerous ground." He turned and walked away.

Was it a threat, or a well-meant warning? Nancy

could not make up her mind. Although Dave was gruff, Nancy liked his straightforward manner.

"I must tell Aunt Bet about this," the young sleuth thought.

The ranchwoman and her nieces were disturbed to hear about the missing bottle, but Mrs Rawley commented with a smile, "The thief must have hated himself for his trouble when he found out there was nothing in the bottle!"

"That's right," Bess agreed. "But he'll go on looking for green bottles and he just may find the right one before Nancy does."

Her detective friend grinned. "Let's not give him a chance!"

As the girls changed to riding togs, Aunt Bet told them of a ghost town on Shadow Mountain. "It's possible Mr Bursey lives there," she said. "You might go to it first, then circle round and on the way back visit the cabin where you think the dog is." She drew a map, then warned, "Be back by sundown. Mountain trails are treacherous after dark."

Nancy took her pocket compass and the girls picked up the lunch Mrs Thurmond had packed for them. Then they hurried to the stable.

Tex gave them the same horses they had ridden the day before, plus a large roan mare named Choo-Choo for Alice. But when the slender girl was astride, she began to giggle.

Tex, too, chuckled. "I don't think I can shorten those stirrups enough for you, Missy," he said. "We'd better put you on a smaller animal."

Bess volunteered to give Alice the horse she was about to mount and the switch was made.

"Choo-Choo's a perfectly good trail animal," Tex said. "Only thing is, she's no river horse."

"I'll remember," said Bess.

With Nancy in the lead, the riders cut across the big meadow at a gallop and started up the mountain trail. Nancy followed Aunt Bet's map, and after a long, hot climb, the girls sighted a group of weather-beaten wooden buildings clinging to the slope above.

As they rode into the streets of the ghost town they were struck by the silence and the bleached look of the sagging buildings. In front of a dilapidated hotel they dismounted and tied their horses to an old hitching rail. As they stepped on to the wooden sidewalk, Alice exclaimed sharply:

"Look!" In front of her lay a crushed blue crayon. "It's a pastel!"

Nancy dropped to her knees and examined the coloured powder. "This is fresh," she said with excitement. "It hasn't been scattered by the wind or mixed with dust."

Beyond the vivid splotch she saw smaller traces of blue and followed them swiftly to the end of the street. Below her, on the rocky mountain slope, she saw two men running.

In a moment they disappeared into a cluster of large boulders. Alice and the others dashed up behind Nancy just too late to see them. Though the girls watched, the men did not reappear.

"I just know one of them was my father," Alice moaned. "He must have dropped the crayon. Oh, Nancy, why do you suppose they ran away? Do you think he's a captive?"

"I don't know yet," Nancy replied. "But I mean to find out."

"Come on. Let's search the town," George urged. "We'll see if there's any sign of an artist living here. If he is, he'll come back."

Alice agreed, and the four separated in order to cover the ground more quickly. Nancy picked a tall house perched precariously halfway up the slope. She entered cautiously and found the ground-floor rooms bare. Gingerly she climbed the rickety stairs.

In the front room she found only a broken brass bedstead. Casually she looked out of the window. On the ground was the long shadow of a man with a big hat! Apparently he was standing round the corner of the building.

Nancy ran to another window and saw the shadow moving towards the rear. She hurried to the back of the building and looked out on to a steep rocky slope. Suddenly among the big boulders on the hillside she spotted a climbing figure in a black ten-gallon hat.

Nancy's heart pounded. Was he the man from Tumbleweed? Did he know she was in the building? If, as she suspected, he was part of the plot at Shadow Ranch, he may have come here to ambush the girls!

"Perhaps I can turn the tables and find out what he's up to," she said to herself. But Nancy realized that she might be cornered in the old building and knew she must get out.

Quickly she started down the shaky stairs. Suddenly there came a rumble, growing louder. For an instant Nancy thought it was thunder, and paused, then she realized the truth.

"A rockslide!" she cried out, but the words were lost in the roar as the entire building was jolted from its foundation!

Escaped Dog

NANCY lurched against the balustrade. Trying to catch her balance, she grabbed the rail. With a loud crash the whole framework broke and she plunged through to the floor below! Stunned, Nancy hardly noticed that the roar of the rockslide had subsided and the old building had come to a shuddering halt. After a while she became aware of voices calling.

"Nancy! Nancy, are you in there?" came Bess's frantic voice.

"I see her!" George's deeper tones were coming closer. As Nancy managed to sit up, she saw that the floor now slanted steeply downhill, and her friends were crawling up towards her.

"Oh, Nancy, are you all right?" Bess asked anxiously.

Nancy managed a shaky smile. "I think I'm just bruised. Now that I've caught my breath, I'll be fine."

George and Bess helped her to her knees.

"We'll have to crawl down," said George. "And the sooner the better. This building might start to slide again."

Nancy and her friends held their breath and gingerly crawled backwards down the slanting floor to the door. The sill was now almost waist-high. As they climbed out, Nancy saw that the building had slipped down to the road.

Alice, carrying a coil of rope, came hurrying up to them. "Oh, Nancy, thank goodness you're all right!" she exclaimed. She explained that George had sent her back to the horses for the rope in case they needed it.

Nancy looked uneasily up at the rocky slope behind the wrecked house. She squinted her eyes against the glare of the sun but could detect nothing moving.

"What do you think caused the rockslide?" George asked.

Nancy told the girls of having seen the man in the black hat. "Maybe he started a boulder rolling," she suggested.

"On purpose?" Bess asked, horrified.

"Perhaps," said Nancy. "I have a feeling it's the same man George and I saw in Tumbleweed. If he's after Valentine's treasure, this is one more move to scare us off the ranch."

George reminded her that no doubt there were other men in the county with large black hats.

"I know," Nancy admitted. She wondered whether the man had followed them there or had been disturbed by their coming.

The other girls said that so far they had found no signs of anyone living in the abandoned village. At Nancy's suggestion they started down the street and, without entering, looked into the few buildings that they had not already checked.

All the while Bess kept glancing over her shoulder to see if anyone was following them. When they reached the end of the street, she and George peered into a tumbledown blacksmith's shop.

Suddenly there was a rustling noise. Bess jumped back and squealed as something scurried past her.

"Really, Bess," George said in disgust, "you're hopeless. That was only a rat."

Bess blushed. "I can't help it. I keep expecting the man in black to jump out at us."

Nancy spoke up. "I think Bess has a point. We'd better get out of here. If the man is still around he just might cause another rockslide."

In a few minutes the girls had mounted their horses and were riding out of town.

"Are we going straight to the cabin now?" Alice asked anxiously. "Perhaps the men we saw were on their way to it."

"Yes," said Nancy. As soon as they were clear of the dilapidated buildings she reined in and studied the map Aunt Bet had given her. After consulting the compass, she led the girls around the back of Shadow Mountain on a narrow trail. Now and then they passed a tall, creamy yucca flower in bloom or startled a bird from a thicket of chaparral. But they saw no other living creatures.

Near noon the riders reached a level place where a cluster of high rocks cast shade over a shallow stream. Here they dismounted, watered their horses, and ate lunch. An hour later the girls were in the saddle again and presently rounded a rock outcrop. They found themselves looking up at a small cabin set among the rocks some distance from them. As the horses climbed towards it, their iron shoes rang against the rock and some of the loose stones clattered down the hill behind them. Suddenly a dog began to bark, then stopped.

"That sounded like Chief!" Bess exclaimed.

While still some distance from the cabin, the riders dismounted.

"Bess and Alice, will you stay with the horses?" Nancy requested. "George and I will take a look round."

The two girls walked stealthily up the hill and started to circle the cabin. They found that the rear wall was close to the side of the mountain and heavily overgrown with brush and small fern. There was an open window in the back wall, but a heavy sack was hanging across it so the girls could not see inside. They stood still for a moment and listened, but no sound came from within. Quietly they completed the circle and returned to the others.

"The door's open a little bit," Bess said softly. "Do you think anybody's inside?"

"There's only one way to find out," Nancy said with determination. "I'll go and knock."

As she started up the hill, the barking started again. The next instant, from behind the cabin, bounded a large black German shepherd dog.

"Chief!" the girls exclaimed.

The dog greeted them with frenzied barking and tail wagging. A short piece of rope hung from his collar. On his head was a swelling and broken skin.

"You poor old fellow!" said Nancy. She knelt beside the dog and calmed him, then carefully felt around the wound. "Someone knocked him out and has been holding him!" she said.

"But why?" asked Bess, keeping a wary eye on the cabin.

"Maybe because he got too close to the phantom horse," Nancy replied.

George looked puzzled. "What difference would that make? Chief can't talk."

"But maybe there's a clue on him—something to show how the trick was done," Nancy replied. The big dog stood patiently as Nancy examined him, but she found nothing unusual.

Bess volunteered to stay with the horses and the dog while the other girls went to the cabin. The trio walked up to it and Nancy knocked on the door. There was no answer. She knocked again, then pushed the door open cautiously.

The one-room cabin was empty, but plainly had been lived in. On the table stood two mugs and a coffee-pot.

Alice darted forward with a cry. Beside the cups lay an unfinished drawing and a pastel crayon.

"My father! He's been here!"

The mugs were half full of coffee. Nancy felt them. They were still warm.

"The artist and his companion have been here, all right," Nancy agreed. "And they left just a short time ago."

"Why would they do that?" George asked. "Unless they heard us coming and have some reason to hide."

"My father's being held prisoner," Alice said positively. She glanced at the older girls and read their thoughts. "You think he's connected with the phantom mystery because we found Chief here," she accused.

Nancy tried to assure her this was not the case. "Your father is innocent, but someone else occupying this cabin may be connected with the Shadow Ranch mystery."

Leaving the door slightly open as they had found it, the three hurried to report to Bess.

"The men may come back. Let's wait here and see," Nancy suggested.

The girls led their horses behind a pile of large boulders, out of sight of the cabin. Keeping Chief beside her, Nancy hid behind the screen of chaparral with the other girls and watched the cabin.

While they waited Nancy puzzled over the dog's appearance. He had run from behind the cabin, yet minutes before she and George had passed between it and the mountain without seeing or hearing the animal. It occurred to Nancy that he might have been tied up some distance away and broken loose.

But why had he been held? There seemed to be no lead to the phantom on him. "Perhaps it was only because his captor is not averse to stealing a good dog."

The afternoon wore on. It was hotter and increasingly cloudy. The men did not return.

Finally Nancy cast a worried look at the sky. "We must start back before it rains."

Alice begged to stay, but the other girls knew this was not wise. Nancy promised her they would come again.

With Chief at the heels of Nancy's horse, the girls started down the mountain, following a path which the River Heights visitors soon recognized as the trail they had been on the day before.

"So this path to the cabin is not impassable, after all," said George, "as Shorty had claimed."

Nancy remarked that the cowboy might have been mistaken, yet she admitted that his behaviour certainly made him a strong suspect in the mystery.

As the girls rode along, the sun vanished and a chill wind set in. Suddenly a few large drops of rain splattered into the dust. The next moment a downpour descended.

The horses snorted. A vivid flash of lightning split a

fir tree some distance up the mountain and the horses shied at the clap of thunder.

"Sit tight!" Nancy called over her shoulder, "and keep moving."

Moment by moment, the cloudburst worsened and the trail gradually became slippery mud. Far below in the valley they could see the sunlit meadow, untouched by the storm.

"I hope we make it," Bess said fearfully.

Suddenly Nancy had a chilling thought. They still had to negotiate the stream which they had crossed the previous day. And Bess's mount was not a river horse! She dare not urge her own mount faster, for the animal was picking his footing carefully. Yet, with each precious minute, she knew that the stream was rising.

When they reached its bank the four girls gazed in consternation at the rushing water.

"We can't cross that!" Bess wailed.

Nancy said the only alternative was to stay all night on the mountain. "And we're not equipped to do that. It's too risky. Come on, Bess. We can make it if we hurry!"

As she spoke, Chief whined and put his paw into her stirrup.

"He's begging for a ride," George said.

The dog leaped to a large rock beside the water and Nancy pulled up close to him. With her help Chief squeezed on to the front of the saddle and Nancy held him there.

"All right, boy," she whispered to him. "Here we go!"

She gathered the reins firmly and guided her horse into the water. The big animal did not fight the current, but swam along easily with it, heading gradually for the opposite bank. Before long, he found footing. As he clambered safely ashore, Chief jumped off and Nancy turned in the saddle to see how the others were faring.

One by one the big, dependable river horses made the crossing safely, but Bess, on Choo-Choo, was last. Would he behave? The animal entered the stream and walked until the water swirled around his shoulders. Then he stopped.

"If he doesn't swim he'll be swept away!" George exclaimed.

"Help!" called Bess. "He won't move!"

With the torrent rising fast, Nancy spurred her mount along the bank until she was some distance above Bess. Then she guided her horse into the turbulent water.

"Hold on, Bess! We're coming!"

Suddenly, a few yards upstream, part of the muddy bank collapsed, sending a huge surge of water sweeping over Nancy and her horse!

· 9 ·

Tack Room Prisoner

KEEPING a firm grip on the reins, Nancy stuck tight to the saddle. In a few moments her mount steadied himself and began to swim towards Bess's horse. When they drew close, Nancy seized Choo-Choo's reins. While the frightened girl clung to the saddle, her horse was towed to shore.

"Oh, Nancy!" she exclaimed. "You were wonderful. You saved us!"

Nancy still looked worried. "We can't stay here," she said. "We're not out of trouble yet. I'm afraid the trail down is going to be slippery and wet."

George grimaced. "What's the hurry? We can't get any wetter than we are."

The girls looked at one another. Despite the situation, they could not repress giggles. All were drenched and mud-spattered, with water streaming from their hair.

"You're lucky Bud isn't here to see you," George teased Bess as Nancy led the way down the trail.

Bess shivered and made a face at her cousin. "I know I must be a sight," she said. "I can tell by looking at the rest of you."

The joking had served to relieve the tension and now the girls applied themselves to guiding their horses down the precarious trail. As they reached the bottom, the rain stopped, and the sun emerged hot and bright.

From there, the trip was easier. By the time they reached the big meadow, their clothes were almost dry.

Chief raced ahead to the stable, barking madly. Bess groaned. "Oh, he's making so much noise he'll bring out a reception committee and everybody'll see us!"

Nancy smiled at the remark, then warned the others to say nothing about the man in the black ten-gallon hat or the other two men to anyone except the Rawleys.

When the girls rode up to the corral, Dave and Tex and Bud were waiting there for them.

"Where did you find Chief?" asked Dave. He surveyed their bedraggled condition but made no comment.

Tex said, "Looks like you girls got caught in a little mountain sprinkle."

Bud grinned and said, "That was nothing. Wait till you all get caught in a real Western-style rain."

"No thanks," Bess retorted.

"We'll tell you all about the dog later," Nancy promised. The girls hastily dismounted and fled to the house.

After hot showers they dressed for supper. Nancy wore a powder-blue sweater and skirt, and brushed her titian hair until it gleamed. George wore a smart dark-green linen dress. She was ready long before Bess, who wore a yellow sweater and skirt and changed her hair-do three times.

"I want to look extra nice," Bess said, "to make up for the awful sight I looked this afternoon."

Before supper, the girls sat down in the living room with the Rawleys and told them of their afternoon's adventures. Nancy passed lightly over the stream-crossing incident, but Bess refused to let the matter drop. When everyone had gathered around the table, she bragged of Nancy's bravery. Nancy, always embarrassed by praise, changed the subject as soon as possible.

When the meal was over, Dave called Nancy aside on the veranda. "I owe you an apology," he said soberly. "That was a mighty fine thing you did this afternoon. I see now that you're not the tenderfoot nuisance I thought you were going to be."

Nancy smiled. "This is the first time since I arrived that you've been friendly. Are you always so gruff to newcomers?"

He flushed. "No, but I—" He hesitated. "Well, I had a special reason."

Before Nancy could ask him what it was, he said, "I have to go now. We'll talk again later."

Dave swung off the veranda and headed towards the corral. Nancy watched him disappear into the dusk, puzzled by his remarks. Was he guilty of something or not? She was aware that Ed Rawley trusted him. On the other hand, she had no proof that Dave had been telling the truth about the mud on his shoes.

She reminded herself that he knew about Frances Humber's watch and therefore had a reason to trick the girls out of their room and later take the old green bottle.

"Did Dave apologize in order to allay my suspicions of him?" she wondered.

As Nancy started towards the living room she met the other girls and Aunt Bet coming out.

"We're going to a drive-in movie," said Alice. "Want to come along?"

"I'd love to," Nancy replied, "but I think I'd better stay at home and keep watch." Bess and George offered to remain with her, but Nancy urged them to go on.

As Mrs Rawley and the girls walked towards the estate car, Nancy hurried to her bedroom. She changed into riding clothes, picked up a torch, and then headed for the stable. She had decided to saddle her mount and be ready to ride in case the phantom horse should appear. The young sleuth was determined to catch the ghost horse or examine its tracks before they were obscured by other pursuers.

As Nancy reached the stable, Dave came out leading a horse which he mounted at once. He carried a torch. "Just checking up," he said to her. "Snooping again?"

"Yes," Nancy replied. Quickly she changed the subject by asking whether anyone kept watch in the big meadow at night for the phantom.

"No," was the reply. "Shorty and I have the first patrol, while Tex keeps watch on the windmill and Bud stands guard at the east meadow. When it's their turn to ride patrol, Shorty and I will switch jobs with them."

He added, "The foreman is riding fence in the east meadow—we even have to do it at night now. That way the cattle will be guarded twenty-four hours a day."

Dave rode off and Nancy went through the stable into the tack room, a long frame building attached to it. She turned on her torch and saw rows of saddles hanging from the walls and bundles of blankets stacked on shelves.

After crossing the room, she lifted one of the saddles from the wall. Above it hung a bridle and bit which Nancy also took down, then she picked up a saddle

"I must get out of here!" Nancy thought desperately

blanket. Turning back, she was surprised to see that the door was closed.

Nancy hurried over, put her gear on the ground, and tried the door. It was locked! She remembered having seen a padlock hanging loose in the hasp outside. Had someone locked her in by mistake?

Nancy pounded on the door and shouted, but no one came. Suddenly she realized that under the guard system no one would be within hearing distance of her voice. Grimly Nancy wondered if Dave had locked her in. Had he guessed her plan and done it to foil her?

"I must get out of here!" Nancy thought desperately.

She played her torch round the long room and saw one window high in the wall. "I can squeeze through, if I can find a way to reach it."

At one end of the room Nancy placed a pile of blankets under the window. Then she stacked saddles on top until she was sure of reaching the window.

Nancy climbed the unsteady pile and tried to push up the sash. The window was locked. She found the catch and managed to turn it. Once again she tried to open the window, but it was stuck tight. Disappointed, she made her way down to the floor.

"Maybe I can find a pole and force the window up," she thought.

Her torch revealed an iron crowbar in one corner. She dragged it back beneath the window, climbed up again, and tried to force the sash open. As she struggled with it she could see the kitchen end of the house and the spring house.

Suddenly the window budged, and at the same moment, Nancy saw a gleam of light through a crack in the spring-house wall. With a gasp of surprise she let the crowbar fall, climbed out of the window, hung for a moment from the sill, then dropped several feet to the ground.

As she hit the earth there was a sharp yelp to her left, and Chief ran towards her, barking loudly. "Hush!" Nancy said.

She patted the dog and tried to quieten him. "Stay here," she ordered, and he sat down obediently while Nancy ran towards the spring house.

When she was halfway there, the light went out. As she reached the door, Mr Rawley came running from the kitchen end of the house.

"What is it, Nancy? What's the matter?" he asked.

Quickly she told him what she had seen. "No one came out," she concluded.

"Then whoever had a light there must still be inside," he declared, and pulled open the heavy wooden door.

Nancy shone her torch inside. The spring house was empty!

· 10 ·

Hidden Entrance

"I just can't believe it!" Nancy exclaimed. "No one could have come out. I could see the door all the time I was running towards it."

Ed Rawley looked at Nancy. "I'm sure you didn't imagine seeing the light. This worries me."

Nancy told him of the similar experience she had had the day before. "Perhaps there's a secret exit," she suggested.

Using her torch, Nancy examined the walls of the spring house, but found they were solid adobe. It occurred to her that there might be a wooden trap door and a passageway under the earthen floor. She looked for any sign of seams in the earth. There were none. Nancy gave a baffled sigh and glanced at the stone vat.

"No use bothering with that," said Mr Rawley. "It's too small to hide in and too heavy to be moved in a hurry. Whoever escapes from here does it in a twinkling."

As Nancy and the rancher left the spring house, she gazed uneasily towards the meadow. "The last time I saw the light, the phantom horse appeared out there," she remarked.

"I'll alert my men to watch for more sabotage," Uncle Ed said quickly. "And I'll take one off patrol duty to stand guard here at the spring house all night."

He hurried away. Nancy stood watching the dark meadow, puzzling over the problem of the disappearing light. The phantom horse did not appear and finally she returned to the house.

Nancy went to the living room, lit a lamp, and sat down alone to think over the mystery. How could someone disappear from the spring house without using the exit? Suddenly she remembered that a prowler had done the same thing from the cellar of the house.

Nancy jumped up excitedly. "Of course that's the answer," she told herself. "The spring house is next to the kitchen and the cellar is under it! There must be a hidden passage from one to the other."

She hastened out of the house and turned the corner, then stopped short. A shadowy figure was lounging outside the spring house. It was Dave on guard. Nancy decided against examining the spring house again that night.

On the way back she glanced into the kitchen. Mrs Thurmond was seated at the big table, reading a magazine. Next to her was Bud Moore. He saw Nancy at the door.

"Howdy," he said. "Mr Rawley changed me into a house guard tonight, so you gals can sleep easy."

"That's great. Thanks."

Nancy smiled, but inwardly she was disappointed. "Now I can't investigate the cellar, either," she thought, "with Bud around."

Nancy woke at dawn. She dressed quickly and slipped out of the house. To her relief, there was no longer anyone on guard at the spring house. She stepped inside and walked to the kitchen wall. Nancy lifted the lid of the vat and looked in. It was empty.

She knelt and began to feel the bottom of the vat. Along the front edge her fingers suddenly encountered a piece of cord and opposite it another piece. Nancy pulled on them and the bottom moved. As she yanked harder, the floor of the vat lifted a few inches. It was made of wood, which had been covered with grey plaster to look like stone!

Before Nancy could lift it higher, she heard footsteps outside. Quickly she dropped the bottom and closed the vat. She had just time to grab a tin cup and hold it under the stream of water before the wooden door opened. Nancy turned and saw Shorty standing there.

For a moment he was speechless with surprise. "Wal," he exclaimed, "you're sure up mighty early, miss!"

"Yes, I am," Nancy said with a smile, then excused herself and left the spring house. As she strolled off, she could feel Shorty's eyes on her.

Nancy knew that the ranch hands rose early. "Did Shorty intend to get a drink of water? Or did he see me go in and come to find out what I was doing?"

Excited by her discovery in the spring house, Nancy could hardly wait for her friends to waken so that she could tell them about it.

At the news George sat up straight in bed. "That's something!" she exclaimed. "You've found the secret entrance to the cellar!"

"I *think* so," Nancy replied. "It was still kind of dark and I raised the bottom only a few inches. There just might be a hidden compartment under the false floor. Let's not tell anyone until we're sure."

Bess said, "Good idea."

The girls dressed in jeans and shirts, hoping to

investigate the mysterious vat very soon. But at breakfast Foreman Sanders ruined the plan.

"Two of the men will be working on the pump most of the day," he announced. "It hasn't been right since the damage was done."

Before the meal was over, Nancy asked with a smile, "Who locked me in the tack room last night by mistake?"

There was silence in the kitchen. Nancy learned nothing. No one wore a guilty expression.

During the morning Mr Rawley asked the four girls if they would like to go with him to Tumbleweed. They all accepted eagerly and piled into the estate car, with Dave at the wheel.

On the way, Uncle Ed told them he was going to the stockyards to pick up a dozen fine palominos for breeding. He had ordered and paid for the horses some time before. "It's a big investment." He frowned. "I just hope nothing happens to them."

Dave drove straight through town and parked on the outskirts in front of the stockyards. As Nancy got out of the car she noticed a sign on the fence: TUMBLEWEED RODEO. BARBECUE AND SQUARE DANCE. SATURDAY.

Dave called her aside. "Will you go to the barbecue and square dance with me?"

Surprised, Nancy hesitated for a moment.

"Please do," he added earnestly. "Bess and George promised Tex and Bud they would go. We can make it a triple date."

"Okay. Thank you," she replied.

"Good," he said, then excused himself and hurried into the stockyard after Uncle Ed.

Meanwhile, the girls walked round the enclosures,

looking at the animals. The visitors were attracted to a small corral where a man was offering trained horses for sale. The girls walked to the fence and joined the cowboys and ranchers who were watching a little chestnut mare perform.

Her master stood in the centre of the ring and gave various whistles. In response the horse pranced, reared, and kneeled. At the final whistle the mare ran to him and took a piece of sugar from his hand.

"Isn't she a darling?" Bess murmured.

As the girls strolled away they saw Dave near one of the horse enclosures. Nancy asked him if she had time to take Bess, George, and Alice to Mary Deer's shop.

"Sure," he replied. "Go ahead. We'll pick you up there in the car."

The girls walked down Main Street and turned into the gift shop. A tall man was standing at the counter, talking to Mary. As he turned round, Nancy stopped short in surprise. He was the man in black she had seen near the shop after the attempted robbery!

Mary greeted the girls warmly and Nancy introduced Bess, George, and Alice. The Indian girl presented the tall man as Mr Diamond, one of her best customers.

He smiled at Nancy smoothly. "Miss Drew, I congratulate you. Mary tells me that she has given you that pretty little antique watch I have had my eye on. For weeks she has been refusing to sell it to me."

Mary spoke up. "I told Mr Diamond the history of Valentine and his treasure," she said. "Ever since then he has been most eager to have Frances Humber's watch."

Mr Diamond gave a deep chuckle. "I like to collect mementos of the romantic Old West."

"Do you live round here?" George asked.

"No, ma'am. I'm spending the summer in this area for my health. Staying at the Tumbleweed Hotel."

Mary smiled. "Mr Diamond spends most of his days riding in the mountains for exercise."

Nancy's thoughts went to the man in the black hat she had glimpsed in the ghost town—the one who perhaps had caused the rockslide. Had it been Mr Diamond? Nancy thought it possible, because of his knowledge of the treasure.

After chatting for a few minutes, Mr Diamond said, "Well, goodbye now, girls," and left the shop.

While the others selected a few souvenirs, Nancy took Mary aside and asked her if she had heard from the artist, Mr Bursey. When Mary said no, Nancy added, "If you do, please phone me right away." Mary promised that she would.

Dave pulled up in the car, so the girls hurriedly paid for their purchases and left.

"The horses are going to be delivered this afternoon," Uncle Ed said with satisfaction as they drove back to the ranch. "They're first-rate animals."

The estate car arrived home just as Mrs Thurmond was ringing the triangle for lunch. Nancy wondered how she would endure the long afternoon waiting for darkness so that she could investigate the vat in the spring house. Her attention was distracted, however, by vans bringing the new horses. The girls and Aunt Bet went outside and watched the men run the palominos into the big meadow.

Nancy hurried to the fence for a closer look. "Oh, they're just beautiful!" she cried out.

Dave, who was on horseback beside the meadow

gate, agreed. "They're just the way they should be—the colour of a new-minted gold coin."

The last one, a little mare, trotted into the enclosure. Dave wheeled beside her and herded the pony to the fence. "Want to pat her?" he asked Nancy.

With a smile Nancy stroked the sleek nose of the palomino. The mare whinnied and shook her head.

Dave laughed. "Okay, little lady," he said, "on your way." He slapped the pony on the rump and she ran off to join the others. With a wave to Nancy, Dave rode off.

She admired the confident way he did his job and his kind, firm manner with the animals. "I do hope he's not mixed up in the mystery." She sighed.

As soon as it was dusk, Nancy hurried to the stable and saddled her mount in case the phantom horse should appear that night. Then she asked Bess and George to join her and investigate the spring house. Bess inquired if they were going to take Alice along.

"She's writing letters in her room," George said. Not knowing exactly what lay ahead of them, Nancy thought it wise to leave the younger girl behind.

When it was dark, she took her torch and the three girls hastened to the spring house. They went inside and closed the door. Nancy turned on her light, raised the vat lid and, with heart thumping, pulled up the false bottom. A deep hole slanted downwards.

While George held the light, Nancy lowered herself into it and felt her foot touch something solid. She kicked lightly and a wooden panel moved. In a few moments she dropped on to an earthen floor. She was in the cellar! Through the hole came Bess. She landed with a thud.

From above came the noise of the vat lid closing.

A moment later George appeared in the cellar, with her torch turned off.

For a moment they stood listening. A shiver ran up Nancy's spine. She thought she could hear someone breathing in the darkness.

Quietly Nancy took the torch from George and turned it on. The sweeping beam caught a crouching figure in the corner! Dave Gregory!

· 11 ·

A Rewarding Search

DAVE rose to his feet. "Well, Nancy, you caught me fair and square."

She noted the spade at his feet. It looked as though her suspicions about Dave had been right. "Are you digging for treasure?" she asked coolly.

"Yes," he said. "But I'm not pulling the phantom trick or causing the damage around here. Please believe me, Nancy. Let me tell you my story."

George advised, "It had better be good."

Dave said, "My brother and sister and I are the only remaining descendants of Frances Humber. I was born in Buffalo, New York, but our family moved to Phoenix when I was ten. We have Valentine's original will, and have always known the story of his treasure, but never bothered to hunt for it.

"However, since my father's death two years ago, things have been hard with us. I've been working my way through college, but will need more money to help educate my younger brother and sister. So I decided to take a summer job on Shadow Ranch and look for the treasure."

"How amazing!" Bess murmured.

Dave reached into his shirt pocket and pulled out a small piece of paper. In the beam of her torch Nancy saw that it was a faded photograph of a pretty woman. She also noticed that the corner was torn and the picture was just the right size to fit into the watch case!

"This is Frances Humber," she announced.

The cowboy looked surprised. "How did you know?"

Instead of replying, Nancy asked him where he had obtained the picture. He explained that after Frances Humber Dale's death, her friend in Tumbleweed, Miss Phillips, had removed the photograph from the watch and sent it to Frances' children in the east. "It has been handed down in our family since then."

Dave turned the picture over and on the back the girls saw the word "*cellar*", written in old-fashioned script. He told them that the tradition in his family was that the cellar was the location of the treasure.

Nancy was excited at this new clue, but before telling him about the note in the watch, she asked him why he had not told Ed Rawley what he was doing.

"I was afraid he wouldn't hire me. He might have thought I'd spend all my time searching." The cowboy assured Nancy that he had done all his treasure hunting in off-duty hours.

"How did you know of the secret entrance?" Bess asked.

"Stories about that have always been known in my family," Dave answered. "Originally the trees grew thickly around the spring house, and in times of Indian attack the occupants would escape by the secret exit into the woods and go to a hideout on the mountain slope."

Dave confessed that he was the prowler who had alarmed Mrs Thurmond in the kitchen. He had hoped to search for the treasure in the cellar that night just after his turn on guard duty.

"But you raised such a rumpus," he said to Nancy with a grin, "that I knew it was no use to go on. I sneaked out through the spring house and came round to the kitchen a little behind the rest of the crowd."

"I believe you, Dave," said Nancy. "But you must promise to tell Mr Rawley first thing in the morning what you have been doing."

The cowboy assured her that he would. "I'm sorry I was kind of rude to you girls. I just didn't want you hanging around and getting in the way of my treasure hunt."

"You were pretty awful," said George. "But maybe we'll forgive you."

"Of course we will," Bess agreed.

Nancy smiled at Dave and he chuckled. "From the start I couldn't help liking you," he said.

Nancy reached into her pocket and brought out the antique watch. She showed him how the secret lid opened. The picture of Frances fitted perfectly to the torn fragment on the empty side.

"You're amazing!" he said. "What a detective!"

Next, Nancy removed the picture of Valentine and turned it over, so that Dave could see what was written on the back.

"With the word on your picture, we now have a complete message!" Nancy said excitedly.

" 'Green bottle in cellar,' " Dave read. "Surely the treasure would be too large for a bottle. But perhaps it's a clue to the real thing."

"That's what Nancy thought," George said, grinning. "Let's start digging!"

For half an hour Dave dug and the girls probed the loose soil for a bottle.

Suddenly Bess cried out. "I've found it!"

Nancy hurried to her side and pressed in the earth where Bess showed her. Her fingers touched the neck of a bottle with a cap on it.

Dave came over and dug carefully round the glass. When it was partly free, Nancy said, "Wait!" She brushed the dirt from the large bottle and shone her light on it. Bess exclaimed in disappointment. The bottle was black.

"No use bothering with that," Nancy said. "We're looking for a green one. This has been lying here for years and gradually became covered with dirt."

With grim determination the treasure hunters continued to dig and sift the earth. When they had worked over the whole cellar floor, the four stopped, exhausted, and sat down.

Bess expressed the thought that was in all of their minds. "Maybe someone has found it already."

"Shorty, perhaps," Dave said. "I've caught him snooping." He told the girls that he suspected the other cowboy of knowing about the secret entrance and of inflicting damage on the ranch. "I'm sure he's not working alone, either, but who else is in league with him I don't know."

Nancy pointed out that if Shorty and his accomplices had found the treasure, they would have left the ranch by this time.

The young detective said, "There's another person who might have found the bottle—Frances Humber herself. What do you know of her story, Dave?"

"Only that Dirk Valentine and Frances had met only once on Shadow Ranch. He sent her a message that he was coming and Frances slipped out of the house through the secret entrance and met him in the spring house. But the law was after Valentine as usual and he had to leave the territory. He wrote to Frances, however, during the summer of 1880, but her father intercepted the letter and sent Frances to friends in Montana.

"Then Valentine probably hid the bottle in the cellar while Frances was away, and sent her the watch with the location of the bottle written on the backs of the pictures."

"That's right," Bess declared. "The date on the watch is June, 1880."

Dave went on to say that Frances must have written to Valentine and told him on what day she would return, for that night the outlaw sneaked on to the ranch to see her.

"But the sheriff and the posse suspected that he would come. They were lying in wait and shot Valentine as he entered the spring house. A few minutes later the sheriff went to the living room to tell his daughter. He found her lighting a lamp. When he told her that her sweetheart had been killed, she fainted."

"Oh, no!" cried Bess.

"For many weeks she was ill," Dave continued. "During this time her father found the watch sent to her by Valentine and took it. When she was well enough to travel, he sent her to stay with relatives in Buffalo. There she married, had two children, and died while still a young woman," he concluded.

George sighed. "Poor thing! She never had a chance to come back here and hunt for her treasure."

Suddenly Dave stood up. "I must go now," he said. "I have to stand watch soon in the east meadow."

Quietly the foursome left the cellar by the secret entrance and parted outside the spring house. The girls went to have a shower and change their clothes.

As Nancy dressed, she mulled over the story Dave had told her. She tried to reconstruct the scene at the ranch house on the night of the outlaw's death.

"If Frances had returned home only that afternoon," Nancy reasoned, "she may not have had a chance to look in the cellar for the bottle until that night. No doubt she also knew or guessed that her sweetheart would come to see her at the place they had met before. When the shots were fired, Frances would surely have heard them."

Here Nancy came to the part of the story that puzzled her. Maybe Frances Humber was in the cellar and ran upstairs to light a lamp? But why? It would have been more natural for her to go outside to be with Valentine. But suppose Frances had already found the bottle? At the sound of the shot she dashed upstairs in a panic, then found that she still had the bottle in her hand.

"Of course! She hid it in the lamp!" Nancy said aloud. "Then when her father walked in, Frances lit the lamp to cover her action."

At the bewildered looks on the faces of Bess and George, Nancy chuckled. Quickly she told them her new theory. "We must ask Aunt Bet if any of the old Humber lamps are still on the premises."

The girls hurried to the living room and found Mrs Rawley seated in a rocking chair, mending her husband's socks. In response to Nancy's question, she told her that there was a lot of junk from former owners in a storeroom next to Alice's bedroom.

The girls hurried down the hall and entered the storeroom. Bess switched on the ceiling light. Amidst old trunks, baskets, and barrels they found a birdcage and a hatstand but no lamp. On the seat of a broken chair lay a ragged quilt with something wrapped in it. Nancy carefully unfolded the bedcover. Revealed was a large oil lamp with a deep ruby glass well.

Bess gave a gasp of excitement, and George said, "If only it's the right one!"

With anxious fingers Nancy removed the chimney and the wick. She reached into the well and pulled out a slender green glass bottle!

Lights Out

"WHAT wonderful luck!" Nancy exclaimed softly. "To think of finding this bottle after all these years!"

"Let's see what's inside it," Bess urged.

Nancy put her little finger into the bottle and slid out a curled-up paper. Carefully she unrolled it, then glanced at the signature at the bottom—a bold "V" and a heart.

"It's a letter from Valentine to Frances," Nancy said.

The girls crowded close and peered at the faded handwriting. The long-dead romance came alive for them as Nancy read aloud:

" 'My dear girl, I am writing this in haste to tell you that I truly love you. Would that we could marry! But the law pursues me and I doubt whether I will live much longer. Too late I am sorry for my misspent life.' "

"How sad!" murmured Bess.

" 'I want you to have my fortune,' " Nancy continued, " 'but many people are seeking it. I know my mail is seized. I have hidden instructions in this bottle. A little of my booty has been converted to gold and melted down into special pieces, dear Frances, made just for you.' "

"I wonder what he meant," said George.

As Nancy was about to read on, the ceiling light

went out. George gave an exclamation of annoyance. "What a time for the bulb to go! Wait here. I'll get one from the kitchen."

As George felt her way out of the room, a suspicion flashed across Nancy's mind. Slipping the letter into her shirt pocket, she said, "Come on, Bess!" and went down the hall with her friend at her heels asking what was the matter.

In the living room Nancy saw the shadowy figure of Aunt Bet standing by a table lamp. "The lights don't work," she said.

At the same moment Alice's voice came up the hall. "Did someone blow a fuse?"

Her fears growing, Nancy groped her way to the telephone and picked it up. The line was dead! She ran her hand down the wire. *It had been cut!*

Nancy returned to the living room as George hastened in from the kitchen.

"No lights there, either," she reported.

"And probably no water," Nancy added grimly. "The pump runs by electricity." She went on to say someone had probably damaged the generator or cut all the wires.

There was a moment of shocked silence.

"But why?" Alice asked in a frightened voice.

"I'm afraid our enemies are about to make more trouble. They think we're helpless without lights or a phone."

"What do you think they'll do?" Aunt Bet asked anxiously.

Nancy said she could not be sure, of course, but she expressed fears about the new palominos.

"We must report this to the men on patrol," said

Mrs Rawley. "They may not yet know anything about the power failure."

Nancy agreed. "But we must be very quiet about it. If the gang doesn't suspect we've guessed their plan, we may be able to catch them in the act."

Nancy suggested that Aunt Bet and Alice keep watch in the house while she and the cousins looked for the guards.

The three hastened to their room to get their torches. "Don't turn them on," Nancy warned, "unless you absolutely have to."

The girls walked out and paused at the edge of the veranda. Somewhere in the darkness men were ready to work more mischief.

"You two go to the east meadow and report to Dave," she said. "I'll locate the palomino guard."

"Be careful," Bess warned. "You may find the troublemakers instead. They struck at the pump house before. Remember? That's close to the big meadow."

"That's why I think they won't do it again," Nancy replied. "Probably they'll pick on a different place. Good luck! If you run into trouble, yell!"

George and Bess melted into the darkness and Nancy hurried in the opposite direction. As she gazed over the fence of the big meadow, she could see most of the palominos standing quietly together near the far end. One or two were browsing in the middle, but there was no sign of a mounted guard.

Quickly Nancy circled the stable and the adjoining tack room, but found no one. Puzzled, she looked across the yard to the corral. It was empty. Where was the guard?

"I must find someone," Nancy thought, but before

she could move, there came a loud whinnying from the stable.

Nancy wheeled and hurried to the door, then paused, well aware that it might be dangerous to go inside. She opened the door quietly and stood listening. Except for the whinnying of a restless animal, all was quiet.

Nancy stepped in and walked cautiously between the two rows of stalls. When she reached the one where her horse stood, it occurred to her that someone might have unsaddled him to prevent her from being first to go after the phantom. But she found the saddle still in place.

As Nancy walked quietly along the left side of the horse, he whinnied nervously. She murmured reassuringly to him and stroked his head. Then she felt the girth to be sure it had not been loosened and ran her hands over the bridle. All was in order.

She was about to leave the stall when there came a loud whinny from the other end of the stable and the sound of a hoof hitting a bucket.

Nancy froze. She heard a footstep!

Suppose it was one of the gang? "If he finds me," she thought, "I'll be trapped in this stall—unable to sound the alarm."

Nancy knew she must try to get out of the stable. The footstep had seemed to be near the excited horse. But exactly where was the intruder now? Nancy slipped out of the stall and, hugging the wall, moved towards the door.

The next moment she was seized from behind and a hard hand stifled her outcry. As Nancy struggled, there came a sharp exclamation and she was suddenly released.

"Nancy!" said a familiar voice. It was Tex! "Great jumpin' steers! I'm sorry! Are you all right?" the cowboy asked anxiously. "Shucks, girl, I thought you were one of the phantom gang!"

Nancy took a deep breath. "I thought you were, too," she said, and quickly told him her news.

The cowboy gave a low whistle. "Trouble's comin', that's for sure!"

"Where are all the guards?" asked Nancy.

"Mr Rawley and Walt Sanders have gone down the valley towards Tumbleweed to watch the road. Mr Rawley figured if outsiders are helpin' to do the damage they might come part way by car, park it, and sneak into the ranch on foot.

"If that's how it's done, maybe he and Sanders can nab 'em. Shorty took early watch, so he's probably sleeping in the bunkhouse.

"I'm set to guard the stable area," Tex went on, "but I figured I'd sure be less conspicuous on foot. A while ago I heard a noise from here and came in to check. It was nothin'—just Daisy thumpin' around. She's restless tonight."

"Who's watching the palominos?" Nancy asked.

"Bud."

"He wasn't a few minutes ago."

"Oh—oh!" said Tex. "Something's wrong there! He'd never leave his post. Come on!"

The two hastened outside. As they turned towards the meadow, from the far end, came a high weird whistle.

The signal for the phantom horse!

Tex stopped short, then raced towards the house, shouting the alarm. Moments later, the clanging of the iron triangle outside the kitchen filled the night.

Nancy, meanwhile, had sprinted into the stable and led out her horse. As she sprang into the saddle, she could see the mysterious glowing steed galloping from the trees into the meadow. It hardly seemed to touch the ground and it wavered in the wind.

"I'm going to catch it!" Nancy vowed, and spurred her horse to racing speed.

Straight ahead lay the meadow gate, but it was closed. Taking a deep breath, Nancy gathered her mount and cleared it.

As before, the phantom was heading straight across the meadow. Nancy rode hard to cut the animal off. She intended to seize the phantom's bridle should it have one on.

In a moment the apparition turned and raced down the meadow, straight towards the palominos. Shrilly whinnying, it plunged into their midst. Some palominos shied and reared, others ran wild.

Nancy's horse, trying to overtake the fleeing phantom, pounded through the scattered group. Suddenly one of the frightened palominos thundered across her path. Frantically Nancy tried to pull her own mount aside.

Too late! The two horses collided. Nancy flew from the saddle and hit the ground so hard she blacked out!

· 13 ·

Missing Artist

WHEN Nancy regained consciousness, Dave was bending over her. "Are you okay?" he asked anxiously, helping her to sit up. "Any bones broken?"

"No," said Nancy. "I guess I'm just bruised. Have I been lying here long?"

"Only a few minutes," Dave replied. "I saw you smack into that palomino and go sailing off. You really reached for the moon!"

Dave lifted Nancy to her feet and steadied her for a moment. As she thanked him, she could hear horses whinnying and men shouting.

"That phantom sure spooked the palominos," Dave said. "Did you get a good look at it?"

Nancy shook her head regretfully. "I didn't get close enough to see how it was rigged."

A horseman reined up beside them. It was Walt Sanders. "Fences have been cut!" the ranch foreman barked. "We've got to round up those palominos. Could take all night or longer if they run into the hills."

He spurred off and Dave turned to Nancy. "Can you make it to the house by yourself?"

"Don't worry about me," she assured him. "I'm fine."

Dave looked around in the darkness, but there was

no sign of Nancy's horse. "I reckon he bolted," he said.

His own mount, a seasoned work animal, stood nearby, unaffected by the panic in the meadow. Dave swung into his saddle. "Keep clear of those running horses," he warned, then rode off after the foreman.

By the time Nancy had walked the length of the meadow to the ranch house, she no longer felt shaken from her fall. In the living room were the three other girls and Aunt Bet. On the table, lighted, was the oil lamp which had belonged to the Humbers. As Nancy walked in, Bess cried, "Did you catch the phantom?"

"Sorry. No."

"Was there any damage this time?" Mrs Rawley asked.

Nancy reported the bad news about the cut fences and the palominos.

Aunt Bet's voice was strained as she said, "If we lose those horses, it will be a crushing blow for us. I appreciate all you've done, Nancy. Bess and George told me how you found the letter."

"It was so clever of you to deduce what Frances Humber did," Alice said admiringly.

"But you didn't finish reading it," George reminded Nancy.

Nancy took the letter from her pocket, smoothed out the paper, and held it close to the oil lamp.

George said, "You left off where he said he had melted down some gold into special pieces."

"Yes, here's the place," said Nancy. She read the next sentence. " 'My treasure is hidden in the oldest dwelling on the ranch.' "

"That's this house," Aunt Bet exclaimed. "We were told that Sheriff Humber built it first."

"Read on," Bess urged. "Exactly where is the treasure?"

Nancy shook her head. "He doesn't say. Listen! 'I fear that I am followed and even this note may fall into my enemies' hands. Therefore, I will say only that you know the place I mean.' "

George groaned. "We'll have to search the whole house. We'd better get started."

"There's likely to be a space under a loose floorboard," said Nancy, "or a niche in a chimney flue, or perhaps a false wall in a cupboard."

She suggested that each of them take a section of the house to investigate.

Nancy herself went to the big fireplace in the living room. She thought that one of the stones in it might conceal a hiding place.

With the aid of her torch the young sleuth tried to peer between the rocks, but they were set close together and no space was visible. She pushed hard on each one, but none budged.

When she finished, Nancy turned her attention to the Indian grindstone. Because it was set in the middle, she thought there might be something special about it and tried hard to move the stone, but it was as tightly in place as all the others.

By the time Nancy had finished checking the living room, the rest of the searchers had straggled back. They reported no success.

Baffled, Nancy suggested that they go to bed. She felt sore and weary. "Maybe I'll be able to think more clearly after I get some sleep." She gave Valentine's letter to Aunt Bet for safekeeping.

At breakfast Uncle Ed was grey-faced and grim.

None of the men had been to bed the night before.

"Six palominos are missing and two are wire-cut," the rancher reported.

Tex snorted, "The meadow fence was wrecked! Some no-good varmint cut it in at least thirty places. We've been workin' on repairs all night. Dave is still out there finishin'."

Uncle Ed announced that he was driving into Tumbleweed to inform the sheriff of what had happened. "Maybe he can spare me a man or I could get some volunteers to help me round up the horses. We'll have to go up in the mountain and look for them. I'll also have the telephone company send a man to mend the wire."

"What about water?" Mrs Thurmond asked.

The rancher replied that the pump and the lights, too, would be working in a couple of hours. "The generator was damaged," he said, "but not seriously."

"The big mischief was the attack on the horses," Nancy remarked. "Whoever planned that wanted to be sure things would be dark and confused and you could not get help in a hurry."

The rancher quickly finished eating and was rising to go when Dave came in. The cowboy asked if he could see the Rawleys alone for a few minutes, and added, "You come, too, Nancy."

Uncle Ed led the way into the living room and closed the door. "Now what is it?" he asked.

Swiftly Dave told the couple about his search for the bandit's fortune. "If I do find the treasure," he added earnestly, "I certainly intend to turn over a share to you both."

Mr Rawley smiled. "Thank you, Dave. But we wouldn't hear of it. I wish you luck."

Aunt Bet now told the men about Nancy's discovery of Valentine's letter.

Nancy pointed out that surely the treasure was linked to the trouble on the ranch. "Until it's found, I'm afraid the phantom horse will continue to appear."

Uncle Ed agreed. "You're a remarkable detective, young lady. Keep up the good work!"

Dave said that with Nancy on the case he thought they had a good chance of finding the treasure. "But I won't be able to do much today. We have those palominos to look for."

Nancy admitted that she did not know exactly where to search next for the hidden treasure.

Aunt Bet patted her shoulder. "You need a holiday from all this trouble. Why don't you girls drive into Phoenix for some fun?"

"That's a wonderful idea!" Nancy said.

As she had thought, her friends were delighted at the prospect. Nancy hurried to get the estate car. When she pulled up in front of the veranda, George was waiting with two vacuum flasks and a jug of water.

As she put them into the back of the car, Dave came hurrying past. He grinned. "I'm glad to see that you tenderfoot gals have turned into water-conscious Westerners."

Alice and Bess were approaching the car and heard him. When he was out of earshot, Alice said, "As for you, Nancy, he's really flipped!"

"And what'll poor Ned do?" George teased.

Nancy grinned. "We'll be home by the time he gets back from Europe."

"Just wait until the square dance tomorrow night," said Bess. "I'll bet Dave's a marvellous dancer."

"I wish," said Alice, "that there was somebody to take me."

There was a gleam in Bess's eye as she said, "Don't give up hope, Alice. You might meet somebody at the rodeo or barbecue."

George looked at her cousin quizzically and Nancy smiled. Both knew Bess loved playing the role of matchmaker!

"What have you got up your sleeve?" George demanded.

"Just my arm," replied Bess, but she grinned.

Nancy spoke up. "Let's do some shopping in Phoenix. I'd like to find something special to wear tomorrow."

"I know," exclaimed Bess. "Let's all buy Indian costumes!"

When they reached the city, George directed Nancy to a shop which sold a variety of Indian apparel and souvenirs. The sight of the colourful squaw dresses drove all thoughts of the ranch trouble from the girls' minds. Happily they tried them on and helped one another make selections. Alice was delighted and pirouetted in front of the long mirror to watch the wide skirts swing out.

Finally Nancy chose a turquoise-blue model with silver rickrack trimming. George's choice was a bold red which set off her short dark hair, and Bess selected one with a yellow skirt and black bodice. Alice picked out a pumpkin-coloured costume trimmed in black.

With their purchases in boxes the girls strolled down the street to a Spanish restaurant. Here they ate a delicious lunch of *tacos* and spicy chilli. For dessert they had iced fresh fruit.

Bess sighed. "Umm, that was super."

Afterwards, they walked to a wide street beside a park where an outdoor painting exhibition was being held. The group stopped now and then to admire and compliment the artists who sat beside their work.

As the other girls lingered over a painting, Nancy wandered ahead, then stopped before a lone picture. After a casual glance she suddenly realized that it was a pastel drawing of the old hotel in the ghost town on Shadow Mountain. Quickly she called her friends.

"That's the same hotel, all right," George declared. "The one where we hitched our horses and found that crushed crayon."

Alice was pale. "My father did that pastel! I know it!" The artist's chair beside the picture was vacant.

"I must find him!" Alice cried out.

· 14 ·

The Nettle Trick

NEAR the empty artist's chair a man sat sketching. Nancy walked towards him. "Pardon me, but do you know where the person is who drew that pastel?"

The man looked up from his work and pointed with his pencil. "There's the one."

Nancy turned and saw a stout woman in a blue dress coming towards them. "Want to buy that pastel, girls? It's the last one. The rest sold like hot cakes."

Alice's face showed keen disappointment. "This isn't your work."

The woman chuckled and sat down heavily. "That's right, dearie. I can't even draw a cow. I'm a dealer. I buy from the artists and sell their work."

"Where is the man who did this picture?" Nancy pressed.

"That I don't know. He told me he was a stranger— just visiting Phoenix. Seemed kind of close-mouthed— didn't say where he came from or where he was staying."

Alice asked, "Was he a slender grey-haired man?"

"Yes. Said his name was Bursey. Do you know him?"

"We think so," Nancy replied.

Alice looked longingly at the picture. "How much is it?" she asked the woman. When Alice heard the price, her face clouded. "I haven't enough money to buy it."

Exchanging quick glances, the other girls reached an agreement. "That's all right, Alice," said Nancy. "We'll make up the difference."

When the picture was paid for, Alice took it gratefully. She thanked the girls as they walked away from the dealer, then added, "Oh, Nancy, you've been so wonderful to me!"

Alice's eyes were misty with emotion. "I feel that we must be getting closer to my father." She thought that he might have returned to the mountain cabin and begged Nancy to go back there with her.

"I wish I could," said Nancy, "but it would be too late to make the trip today after we reach the ranch. Tell you what, though. I'll take you in the morning."

George had another idea. "There's just a chance our Uncle Ross Regor might be around this exhibition somewhere. He might have come to see how his pictures are selling."

The others agreed that George had a point. And for a while the four girls strolled through the park, keeping their eyes open for the slender grey-haired man. They did not see him.

Near mid-afternoon Nancy treated everyone to cool lemonades from a passing vendor and they sat on a bench to drink them. Bess glanced at her watch and suggested they start for home. George drove.

They crossed the desert without trouble and arrived at the ranch in time for supper. At the table they learned that the telephone, lights, and water had been restored, but four of the palominos were still missing.

"The critters are up on Shadow Mountain some-where," Bud remarked gloomily as he passed the biscuits to Nancy. "We have our work cut out to track 'em."

"And we might as well face it," said Uncle Ed, "they might be badly hurt."

To lighten the conversation, Aunt Bet reminded everyone of the barbecue next day. "It's customary for us ranch folks to take a dessert. Any suggestions?"

Tex grinned. "I sure do cotton to chocolate cake."

"Nancy makes scrumptious ones," said Bess.

"Then I guess she's elected," Mrs Rawley said with a smile.

Nancy laughed. "Thank you for the job, my friends! Now, who's going to help?"

"I will!" chorused Dave, Tex, and Bud.

"Good," said Nancy. "You boys can shell the walnuts for topping the icing—that is, if you have any, Mrs Thurmond."

"We have plenty of everything," the cook declared. "Just step right up and take hold!"

"We'll all help," Bess said happily. "Let's make it an extra big cake."

After supper the girls dried the dishes for Mrs Thurmond. Then Nancy put all the cake ingredients on the big kitchen table. The cook gave her several large bowls.

Tex grinned as he picked up a nutcracker. "Boys, we hired out to punch cows and here we are peelin' nuts!"

While Nancy and her assistants worked, they talked

about the phantom. Mrs Thurmond listened intently.

"Where do you think the ghost horse is kept?" Alice asked.

"Folks say Valentine had a hideout on Shadow Mountain," Mrs Thurmond spoke up, "and I figure that's where the critter stays now—same as it did in life."

The girls tried to convince the cook that the apparition was a mere trick, but they could not do it.

Nancy changed the subject. "If Valentine did have a hideout in this area, very likely he kept his horse in a corral there. It's possible that the people who are attacking the ranch have discovered the place and are using it for their trick horse."

Mrs Thurmond shook her head gloomily. "If it was real folks doin' the damage, I'd face right up to 'em," she declared. "But I've seen that spook with my own eyes. I tell you it's too much for my nerves!"

By the time the baking was finished, Mrs Thurmond had excused herself and gone to bed.

"Now for the icing," said Nancy.

When the cake was cool enough, she covered it with thick creamy swirls of dark chocolate and studded the top with whole walnuts.

Bess sighed. "It's too bad we can't have just a teeny piece now, isn't it?"

"I sure could go for a slab," Tex agreed hungrily.

"Come on, cookie," Dave coaxed Nancy.

"Think how good that would taste to us poor riders out on the midnight watch," Bud said in his soft drawl. "Saddlesore, weary—"

"You're breaking our hearts," George said cheerfully.

"Plain biscuits and milk tonight," Nancy announced

"Hang on, Nancy!" Tex shouted

with a chuckle. "You'll get your cake tomorrow."

In the morning Alice could hardly contain her excitement over the trip to the cabin. Not wanting their destination known, Nancy had warned Alice to say nothing of her hopes at the breakfast table. When Aunt Bet asked the girls about their plans, Nancy said, "Alice and I would like to go for a ride in the mountains."

George had letters to write and Bess said she wanted to wash and set her hair.

"I'll saddle up for you," Shorty volunteered. Nancy was surprised at his friendly gesture. She and Alice thanked him, then hurried to change into riding clothes.

When they were dressed and waiting on the veranda, Tex walked up, leading Nancy's bay. Just behind him came Shorty with a sorrel for Alice. Nancy stepped into the yard and mounted easily. With a shrill whinny, the horse reared.

"Hang on!" Tex shouted.

Nancy gripped the pommel tight and hung on to the reins. The horse pitched high and landed stiff-legged on all fours!

Tex seized the bridle and held the bay down, giving Nancy time to fling herself from the saddle.

"Hey, boy! Easy now!" Tex said as he tried to calm the excited animal.

"Nancy, are you hurt?" Alice asked worriedly.

"I'm all right," Nancy replied breathlessly. "But what's the matter with the horse?"

Shorty had hurried to Tex's assistance, and now the snorting steed was standing still. The red-haired cowboy's eyes narrowed with suspicion as he loosened the saddle girth and reached up under the blanket.

"I thought so!" He brought out his hand and held it open for the others to see. In his palm lay a nettle.

Shorty's eyes grew wide. "Well, what do you know about that!" he drawled.

Tex looked at him levelly. "What do *you* know about this?"

"Me!" exclaimed Shorty. "Some mean coyote pulled that trick, not me!"

"You saddled the animals," Tex retorted and turned to Nancy. "I was passin' the stable when Shorty came out with these mounts. He asked me to bring this one over to you."

"Now hold on thar a minute," Shorty put in. "When I went to the stable after breakfast I found this bay already saddled. I throwed the saddle on the other one and brung 'em out. That's all I know about it. You got no call to accuse me. No sir! Not me!"

Tex's face flushed with anger. "*If* you're tellin' the truth, Shorty Steele, I apologize."

Before the stocky cowboy could answer, Nancy suggested that Tex check Alice's saddle blanket. He did and reported that it was all right. The girls mounted and rode towards the meadow.

"I don't believe Shorty was telling the truth," said Alice.

Nancy said nothing, but she was inclined to agree. Aloud she said, "Someone has not given up trying to get me out of the picture."

When they finally sighted the cabin, Nancy reined up behind the clump of big boulders. She swung from the saddle and hitched her horse to a rock, but was not so quick as Alice. The younger girl dashed to the cabin and knocked on the door. As Nancy ran up, it was opened by a slender grey-haired man.

With a shock Nancy recognized him. He was the one who had put the snake's rattle into her knitting bag and dropped the warning note into the car!

· 15 ·

A Perilous Ride

ALICE was on the verge of tears. The man in the cabin doorway was not her father!

He scowled at the two girls. "What do you want?"

Nancy was sure the man must have recognized her, but he gave no sign of it, so she pretended not to know him. Quickly she thought of an excuse for coming. "Are you Mr Bursey?" she asked.

"Yes. Why?"

"We'd like to buy one of your pastels," Nancy replied.

"My what?"

"Pastels—your pictures," Nancy said.

"Oh," The man paused. "I haven't any more. How did you know I was here?"

Nancy explained casually that Mary Deer had told them the artist lived on the mountain. "Several days ago we happened to see this cabin and we thought perhaps it might be where you live."

He gave Nancy a long, hard look. "My paintings are all gone," he said. "No use coming back."

Nancy apologized for bothering him, and as the girls turned to walk back to their horses, he closed the door.

Alice was deeply upset. "I just can't believe that man drew those pictures."

"I'm sure he didn't," Nancy replied as the girls

mounted. "He's no artist. He didn't know what I meant by pastels and he called the pictures paintings. He should have known they're drawings made with special crayons."

She told Alice how she, Bess, and George had encountered the man before.

Alice was excited. "Maybe he's holding my father prisoner somewhere!"

Nancy agreed that was possible. But where? she wondered. There had been no one else in the one-room cabin. Recalling how Chief had appeared mysteriously from behind it, Nancy surmised there was a hiding place nearby.

"What shall we do, Nancy?" Alice asked.

"Report to the sheriff as fast as we can."

Nancy added that if Alice's father was a prisoner of Bursey, the grey-haired man and his pals might very well be the Chicago bank robbers. "And since Bursey is also mixed up with the ranch trouble, his gang is probably responsible for the phantom horse."

As the girls rode down the trail, Nancy's thoughts dwelt uneasily on the man who said his name was Bursey. Could he possibly believe that she had not known him? "I'm afraid my trumped-up story didn't fool him," she decided. "He must know I'll report him to Sheriff Curtis. But why didn't he try to stop me?"

The answer was plain. The man believed that people knew the girls' destination. "He doesn't want us to disappear at his cabin," Nancy told herself, "so he'll arrange an 'accident' for us on the way down the mountain."

She turned in her saddle and warned Alice to keep

alert for signs of pursuit. A little farther along they came to a fork in the trail.

"Let's follow this other path," Nancy suggested.

They soon found the new route a hazardous one, however, and were forced to slow down. The horses were picking their footing on the narrow trail which wound back and forth across a sheer cliff.

Alice glanced up. "Uncle Ed says that Westerners call this kind of path an 'eyebrow trail'. I can see why."

A few minutes later the girls rode under a rock overhang, which prevented them from seeing the turn of the path above them. Suddenly pebbles and dust started falling from above. Someone was following them!

Nancy signalled to Alice, who nodded her understanding. The riders sat in tense silence as their horses slowly proceeded to the bottom of the cliff, where the trail became less steep. But it was narrow and precarious. The girls urged their horses to go as fast as they dared. Soon they heard the clatter of a horse's hoofs behind them.

Nancy knew they had no defence against the surprise attack she feared was coming. It would take only a few boulders rolling from above to scare the horses and cause the "accident".

Nancy looked ahead for shelter. Some distance below, the trail disappeared among high rocks. "If we can reach that spot before our enemy strikes," she thought, "we may have a chance!"

Again the girls urged their mounts on and rode desperately towards the screen of rocks. Jolting hard, Alice clung to the saddle horn all the way.

"We made it!" she gasped as they rounded a curve

and were hidden between huge boulders which lay on either side.

Swiftly Nancy dismounted, signalling her companion to do the same. The younger girl followed as Nancy led her horse into a cluster of the giant rocks. Alice held her mount firmly and kept one hand soothingly upon his nose. If only the animals would stand quietly! One jangle of the bridle, or a hoof scuffing a stone, and their hiding place would be revealed!

Hardly breathing, the girls heard the clatter of stones as their pursuer approached. The sounds came closer, then suddenly stopped.

"He sees we're not on the trail ahead," Nancy thought. Would the rider guess that they had rounded the next curve but were hiding? For a long moment there was silence from the other side of the boulders.

"He's listening!" Nancy thought.

The girls stood frozen. Then came the creak of a saddle and the sound of hoofs as the rider moved on.

Nancy and Alice gave sighs of relief, and, after waiting a few minutes, led their horses out of the boulders. Quickly the two remounted.

Alice said fearfully, "When he reaches open mountainside again, he'll see that he has missed us and come back. We'll meet him head-on!"

"I know," Nancy replied. "We must look for another branching trail."

Presently she spotted a side path among the boulders and the girls guided their horses on to it. The way downwards was narrow and rough, but the two riders were sheltered first by rocks, then by tall fir and tamarack trees. They reached the valley a mile from where the other trail came down.

"We made it safely!" Alice cried in relief. "Oh, Nancy, how can I ever thank you?"

Her companion smiled. "Don't think I wasn't scared myself!"

It was noon when the girls dismounted at the stable. They hurried to the living room where they found the Rawleys chatting with Bess and George.

While Alice excitedly reported all that had happened to them, Nancy telephoned the sheriff. She told him her suspicions of the man calling himself Bursey, and also the possibility that Ross Regor, Alice's father, was being held prisoner on the mountain by the same gang responsible for the phantom-horse trick.

Sheriff Curtis said, "I'll go up to the cabin at once with two men and arrest this hombre Bursey and his confederates."

Nancy hastened back to the living room and reported the conversation.

"That's great!" exclaimed George. "If the sheriff catches the bank robbers, it will mean the end of the damage on the ranch."

"But they must have another hideout, where they keep Uncle Ross," Bess objected, "and we don't know where that is. Besides, the sheriff may find only Bursey."

"But if he talks, we'll get to the bottom of the mystery," Nancy reminded her.

Suddenly the door to the veranda burst open and Dave came in. "Mr Rawley, we found the missing horses!"

Amid the girls' exclamation of joy, the rancher beamed and asked. "Where are they?"

"Tex, Bud, and I put them in the meadow. We found them up on Shadow Mountain, grazing by a creek."

Dave hesitated. "The only thing is, they're hurt."

Mr Rawley's jaw tightened. "Bad?"

"Three of 'em are wire-cut and one mare is limping. We'd better call the vet."

The rancher agreed and Dave hurried to the telephone. "Could be worse," Uncle Ed said. "Maybe everything will be all right—provided there's no more damage."

Aunt Bet smiled cheerfully. "Nothing more is likely to happen. After all, the sheriff is on his way to round up the gang—thanks to Nancy."

In a happy frame of mind, the girls hurried away to dress in their squaw outfits before lunch. While she had a shower, Nancy's thoughts were on the treasure. Where could the outlaw have hidden it? Still puzzling, Nancy slipped into her blue costume. She brushed her titian hair until it gleamed, then put on a pair of small silver earrings and added a touch of lipstick.

The other girls were not ready yet, so Nancy went into the living room to wait for them. As she seated herself in one of the rocking chairs, her glance fell on the fireplace. Once again, the Indian grinding stone caught her attention. She recalled what Aunt Bet had told her about it and about the other stones. Suddenly her eyes lit up with an idea and she jumped forward in excitement.

"Bess! George! Alice!" she called, running to the door.

"What is it?" asked George as the three girls came hurrying down the hall.

Nancy's eyes sparkled with excitement. "I think I know where the treasure is!"

·16·

The Sheriff's Quarry

A BURST of excited questions met Nancy's announcement. She chuckled and George said, "Quiet, everybody. Now tell us where the treasure is."

Nancy led her friends into the living room, shut the door, and announced, "In the cliff houses down the valley."

"They're certainly the oldest dwellings around here," said George. "But they are not on the ranch."

"They were when Valentine wrote his letter."

"Nancy, how do you know?" Alice asked.

"Because Aunt Bet told us that every stone in this fireplace came from somewhere on the ranch. It stands to reason that the Indian grinding stone came from the cliff dwelling." She reminded the girls that Sheriff Humber had been obliged to sell that part of his property after Valentine's death. "It's natural that he would get rid of the outlying section first."

"Nancy," declared George, "that's a great piece of deduction."

Just then the triangle clanged for luncheon. As the girls hurried to the kitchen, Nancy requested them to keep her theory a secret.

"We won't be able to check it before tomorrow, and we don't want anybody else to get there before us."

As the group hurried into the kitchen, they stared in amazement. Mrs Thurmond, ladelling out stew at the stove, was wearing her big white apron as usual, and on her head was perched a black straw hat bedecked with artificial roses. Instead of being amused, the cowboys stood about looking uncomfortable and Aunt Bet's face was strained.

"I'm leavin'!" announced the cook, without turning from her work. "I've fixed my last dinner in this place. As soon as it's over, I'm ridin' into Tumbleweed with you young folks and takin' the three-o'clock bus for Phoenix."

Mr Rawley said soothingly, "Things have been pretty rough around here, Mrs Thurmond. But we think they'll be getting better pretty soon."

Mrs Thurmond faced the rancher squarely. "Mr Rawley, I can take rough times with the best of 'em, but phantom horses—that's too much for me." She picked up the big bowl of stew and walked towards the table.

Aunt Bet followed her, pleading. "Mrs Thurmond, please reconsider."

"Nope!" said the woman, and set the bowl down with a thump.

Nancy knew that the loss of the cook would be an added hardship for Aunt Bet, who not only had ranch-house duties, but was needed to help her husband.

This new crisis threw a pall over the meal. At the appearance of a magnificent lemon meringue pie, the gloom became even deeper, for it seemed likely to be the last time any of the diners would taste Mrs Thurmond's fine baking.

When the dessert was gone, the men pushed back their chairs and rose. Immediately the cook asked Dave what time he would be driving the car to Tumbleweed.

Before he could answer, Nancy spoke up. "Not for half an hour yet, are you, Dave?"

He caught the urgent message in her eyes and nodded. "I'll honk the horn when I'm ready to go," he promised.

As soon as the men had left the kitchen, the girls and Aunt Bet gathered round Mrs Thurmond and pleaded with her to remain. The little woman shook her head regretfully, but steadfastly refused. "That phantom has me scared out o' my skin," she declared.

"If I could prove to you that the phantom is a real horse, Mrs Thurmond," Nancy asked, "would you stay?"

"'Course I would! I'm not afraid of a live critter."

"Then just let me have a little time. I feel sure I'll be able to show you how the trick is done."

The others chimed in, cajoling the cook to give Nancy a chance. Bess added, "I don't know how we'll get along without you and all those wonderful pies."

Mrs Thurmond considered a moment. "All right. One more night." At their delighted thanks she flushed with pleasure and marched off to remove her hat. When she returned, the girls and Aunt Bet helped her clear the table. Before long, the horn of the car sounded and Nancy left with her friends.

Dave, Tex, and Bud were in the yard talking to Uncle Ed. Bud was holding a guitar in a case. A short distance away Shorty lounged against the horse trailer, which had been hitched to the back of the estate car.

As the girls came up, they heard Uncle Ed say, "You go ahead, boys, and have a good time. You've earned a holiday."

"You might need help with those palominos when the vet comes," said Dave. He glanced uneasily at Nancy and she understood at once how he felt.

"I'll be glad to excuse you, Dave, if you feel you ought to stay," she said.

"No, that's not necessary," Ed Rawley said.

As Dave thanked him, Nancy noticed Tex talking quietly to Alice. Flushed with excitement, she smiled happily and hurried to Nancy's side. "Tex's brother Jack is going to be in the rodeo and Tex says Jack would like to take me to the barbecue and dance. He's fifteen—Jack, I mean. Is it all right, Uncle Ed?" she asked, blushing.

The rancher nodded and chuckled. "I've met the young man. Go ahead."

As Alice went back to tell Tex, Nancy and George looked knowingly at Bess, who dimpled.

"Now how did you fix that, Miss Cupid?" her cousin asked.

"It was easy," Bess replied. "I remembered Tex had mentioned his brother was coming into Tumbleweed for the rodeo."

"Come on!" called Tex. "Let's roll!" The others hastened to the car.

Bud, carrying his guitar, climbed into the back of the car, and Shorty joined him. Tex, George, and Bess sat in the middle, while Nancy and Alice took seats next to Dave, who was at the wheel.

"I've never been to a rodeo," Alice said as they started out. "What's it like?"

Tex grinned. "Well, Dave here is going to flip some fancy loops and so's Bud."

"He means they're going to rope cows," said Bess.

"Steers," Tex corrected.

Bess asked Tex what he was going to do. "Dog a steer," was his reply.

Dave chuckled at Alice's puzzled look. "He'll ride his horse alongside a running steer and leap aboard."

"Then he'll bite the dust," Bud teased.

"Not Tex!" Dave rejoined. "He's a real salty bulldogger!"

"And Shorty there is a broncobuster," Tex added.

"And I'm fixin' to win, too," Shorty declared. "Wouldn't be the first time." He went on to brag about several occasions when he had won prizes in rodeos.

While he talked, Nancy was quiet, thinking hard about the phantom horse. "Oh, how I wish Chief could talk!" she said to herself. "He's been closer to it than anyone." She wondered again why the dog had been held prisoner.

Suddenly Nancy thought of the light she had seen in the spring house shortly before the ghost horse had appeared. With a thrill of excitement, Nancy suddenly hit on how the trick could have been done! It was all she could do to keep from exclaiming aloud. She decided to say nothing to the other girls until she had an opportunity to prove her theory. "And I can't do that until after dark," she thought.

When they reached Tumbleweed, Dave drove slowly through the streets crowded with visitors. Many of the men had on fringed buckskin jackets and some of the women wore long pioneer dresses with sunbonnets. Others wore graceful squaw dresses.

Suddenly Nancy spotted a drably dressed grey-haired man standing in the doorway of a store—the man who called himself Bursey! At that moment his eyes met hers and he darted away into the crowd.

Nancy's heart sank. The sheriff, who was on his way to or from the cabin, had missed his quarry!

Nancy wondered what to do—get word to the authorities? Dave interrupted her thoughts by saying that the rodeo would not start for an hour. "We have to go and check in," he said. "What do you girls want to do in the meantime?"

"Oh, we'll keep busy," Nancy replied.

When the cowboys had left, she suggested that Bess take Alice and hunt for Bursey. She and George would go in another direction. "Let's meet at Mary Deer's shop."

They all arrived half an hour later. There had been no trace of the man. "He probably left town in a hurry," George declared.

The store was crowded and Mary Deer had an assistant working behind the counter. While the other girls looked at jewellery, Nancy beckoned her Indian friend aside and asked if she would keep a secret. When Mary promised, Nancy told her that she hoped to find the treasure in the cliff dwellings, and inquired the best way to get to them.

"There are stairs up the front," said Mary, "but they are not safe. You had best come down from above."

She explained that at the far end of the cliff apartments there was a huge slab of rock which had been used as a lookout point by the ancient Indians. Stairs led from the rock down to the top row of dwellings. Nancy thanked Mary and promised to let her know if she discovered anything.

By this time the other girls had bought Indian

jewellery, and after Nancy had purchased a turquoise pillbox hat for Hannah, they left the shop. The four-some followed the arrows to the far end of town where they found the rodeo arena, a short distance from the stockyard. Nancy bought tickets at the front gate, and they all found seats in the stands.

Bess sighed. "I'm so hot, I'd like to have a cold drink and I think I need a hot dog to go with it."

George grinned. "Eating is really a very fattening hobby, dear cousin."

Before Bess could retort, a voice came from the loud-speaker. "Telephone call for Miss Nancy Drew in the booth next to the refreshment stand."

The girls looked at one another in amazement. Afraid that something had gone wrong at the ranch, Nancy excused herself and hurried off. She made her way through the crowd to the first telephone booth beside the hot-dog stand. As she reached it, the door opened and Bursey stepped out with a grin. At the same moment a tall figure in black glided to her side—Mr Diamond!

Bursey's strong fingers closed on Nancy's wrist. "You're coming with us!" he growled. "And don't yell or you'll be sorry!"

·17·

An Interrupted Programme

BEFORE Nancy could say anything to the two men, Bess's voice rang out. "She is *not* going with you!"

"Let her go!" George ordered.

As Bursey whirled in surprise, Nancy jerked her wrist from his grasp. Diamond's startled look changed to a scowl and the two ran away fast, disappearing under the grandstand.

"Girls, you were wonderful!" Nancy exclaimed, recovering from her shock. "But those men must be caught!"

The three friends dashed after the fugitives, all the while looking for a deputy but seeing none. Finally they gave up the chase—the two men had vanished.

"I'll go to the sheriff's office and report this," Nancy said.

"Not alone!" George declared. "We're sticking close to you for the rest of the afternoon. It's a good thing I let Bess talk me into coming down for a hot dog."

Bess thought she had better go back to Alice, who was holding their seats in the grandstand. George accompanied Nancy to Sheriff Curtis' office, where the young sleuth left a note for the absent lawman about the kidnapping attempt.

When they returned to the rodeo arena, they heard a burst of cheering. "Dave just won the roping contest!" cried Alice as Nancy and George took their seats. The delighted girls clapped loudly.

"Bud was good too," Bess put in loyally, as Dave walked to the judges' stand. Modestly he accepted the first prize, a pair of silver spurs, and left the arena to another burst of applause.

Next came the broncobusters. The girls watched, thrilled, as one after another of the contestants hurtled into the arena on the bucking horses.

Shorty came last. Shrill whistles filled the air as he tried to stick in the saddle for the required number of minutes.

"Look at 'im sunfish!" came a shout from the stands as the frantic horse pitched high into the air, his back arched.

Suddenly a shot rang out from the judges' stand. "Time's up! Shorty won!" George exclaimed.

The stands erupted into cheers. At the same time, the bronc shook his rider loose. The winner rolled over in the dust, picked himself up, retrieved his hat and waved it at the spectators. As the bronc was taken out of the arena by attendants, Shorty strode to the judges' stand. He claimed his prize, a silver buckle, and held it up for all to see. Then he swaggered out of the arena.

After the rodeo the girls met their dates outside the front gate. Tex introduced his brother Jack, a tall freckle-faced boy, whose friendly manner immediately put Alice at ease. Quickly Nancy warned the boys about Bursey and Diamond.

Dave looked worried and Jack spoke up. "I don't know what this is all about, but no one will get Alice away from me until I turn her over to Nancy after the dance!"

Nancy and Dave led the way to the car. "Shorty said he'd come along later," he remarked.

On the drive to the barbecue grounds, Nancy quietly told him her deduction about the treasure. Dave was excited and said he hoped she was right.

About a mile beyond Tumbleweed he parked in a grove of willow trees beside a narrow stream. The grounds were set with many long wooden tables and benches, and overhead were strings of small electric lights.

"Come on, gals," said Tex. "We're goin' to put on a big feed!" He led them towards a long serving table. Four men passed by, each carrying a shovel bearing a big canvas-wrapped parcel. These were dumped on to the table.

"There goes the meat," said Bud. "It's been buried in the barbecue pit since last night."

"Cookin' nice an' slow over hot stones," Tex added.

"When the canvas fell away, the fragrance of the steaming meat was irresistible. All the girls enjoyed generous servings, with a spicy sauce and potato salad.

By the time they had finished their desserts of ice cream and Nancy's chocolate cake, the coloured lights overhead came on. A stout middle-aged man mounted the dance platform in the centre of the grove and announced that he was master of ceremonies. Seeing Bud's guitar, he called on him for some cowboy songs.

Bud played "I'm a Lonesome Cowboy", and everyone joined in enthusiastically. He followed with a number of other old favourites. Finally he strummed some Gold Rush songs, including "Sweet Betsy from Pike".

The cheers and applause had not yet died down when Shorty stepped on to the platform. Ignoring the master of ceremonies, he leaned towards the microphone and said, "Folks, how'd you like me to do my imitations?"

At the scattered handclapping and whistles, the stout man nodded and stepped back. Shorty cupped his hands around his mouth, closed his eyes, and the long mournful hoot of an owl filled the night.

"He's really good," Bess whispered.

"I'll bet he can also do a whining dog," Nancy said meaningfully.

Next, the cowboy announced a coyote and produced several realistic howls. Suddenly in mid-howl he spotted Nancy in the audience. His jaw dropped and he stood silent before the microphone. Staring at her, he stammered that his act was over and left the platform. The girls exchanged baffled glances.

Dave grinned. "That was one surprised coyote, all right! He thought his pals had got rid of you, Nancy."

Just then a band of three musicians began tuning up and a square-dancing contest was announced. Alice suggested that the four couples enter as a set, and the others agreed enthusiastically.

Of the four groups in the contest, Nancy's was called first. The young people lined up on the platform, facing each other in couples. At the sound of the lively music they began to dance. The fiddle player called the steps and played his tunes fast.

"Swing your partners and a do-si-do!"

Whirling past the edge of the platform, Nancy glimpsed Shorty glowering at her.

When the breathless dancers returned to their table, Nancy told the others of the incident. "It's going to be hard to shake Shorty from now on. I'm afraid he and his pals will watch us so closely we'll have no chance to go after the treasure."

While the other sets of dancers competed, Nancy pondered on how to make sure the girls were not followed to the cliff houses.

At the end of the contest, the crowd voted by applause and the Shadow Ranch group won easily. Nancy was sent to the platform to claim the prize.

The master of ceremonies handed her a pink slip of paper. "You take this to the food table over yonder, young lady, and they will give you and your friends a big ice-cold watermelon!"

Nancy thanked the man, then turned to the audience and said, "I would like to make an announcement that I believe will interest everybody in this area. My friends and I think we know where the famous long-lost Valentine treasure is hidden."

An excited rustle ran through the crowd and cries of "Where?"

Nancy smiled. "I won't say anything more about it now, but tomorrow a few Shadow Ranch men are going out to do some digging."

As Nancy hurried from the platform, she saw Sheriff Curtis making his way towards her. He spoke of his futile search on the mountain and his regret that the desperadoes were still at large. "I'm sure glad you outwitted 'em this afternoon. Watch your step."

Then he joined the young people at their table.

George asked Nancy, "What was the meaning of that announcement you made?"

In a low voice the young detective said, "Everybody look happy—not as if we're talking about anything important—and I'll explain."

Dave obligingly gave a broad grin. "I'll collect our prize."

He soon returned and began cutting and serving the watermelon. Meanwhile, the others listened, smiling and laughing as Nancy told them that the Shadow Ranch cowboys were to act as decoys while the girls went to the cliff dwellings to search for the treasure.

"Shorty will no doubt alert Bursey and Diamond and they'll be keeping an eye on the ranch."

Sheriff Curtis praised Nancy for her plan and said he would follow the decoy group. "I'll nab the varmints when they move against the cowboys."

His blue eyes were sober as he said, "I can see you're a capable gal, Miss Drew, but you've got to be extra careful from now on, 'cause those thievin' hombres'll want to keep all o' you tenderfeet quiet."

"We'll stay close to the girls," Dave promised, and the cowboys permitted no one to cut in during the dancing that followed.

When the party was over, Jack said good night to Alice at the ranch wagon and promised to telephone her soon. As Nancy and her friends climbed into the car, Shorty came hurrying up to join them.

Dave drove to the corrals behind the arena where Tex and Bud coupled up the horse trailer. Shorty got out, too, and walked into a phone booth at the edge of the parking area. He did not stay long.

"I'll bet he called Diamond and Bursey to tell them what I said," Nancy declared.

As Dave started the drive home, Shorty questioned Nancy about her announcement. She laughed and replied that he would see later what she meant. Before he could ask any more questions, Bud struck a chord on his guitar and started a cowboy song. Shorty gave up talking and sat sullenly while the others sang all during the ride.

Although she joined in the songs, Nancy's thoughts dwelled on the plan she had made for proving to Mrs Thurmond that the phantom horse was a trick. She was pleased to note that the moon had gone behind heavy clouds and the night was very dark.

When they reached the ranch, the cowboys hurried off to relieve Ed Rawley and the foreman who had done guard duty during their absence. The girls went to the house where they found Mrs Rawley in the lighted living room. Chief lay by the fireplace.

"I felt safer with him in here," Aunt Bet explained.

Nancy asked the others to accompany her to the kitchen. There they found Mrs Thurmond seated at the big table reading a magazine.

"I believe I can show you now how the phantom was made to appear," Nancy said.

The cook looked sceptical, then exclaimed nervously as Nancy turned out the lights. With a mysterious smile, she slipped outside and hurried down the veranda. Soon she returned. "All set? Look through the screen door."

Her friends complied and stared into the darkness. Suddenly Mrs Thurmond gave a scream and Mrs Rawley gasped. Bobbing towards them, about three feet above the veranda, were tiny glowing specks!

"Oh!" moaned the cook. "Phantom spots! Take 'em away!"

Nancy opened the door and the shining specks floated into the room!

18

The Black Phantom

As the watchers stared amazed, the glowing specks stopped moving and hung in the darkness.

"Oh!" Mrs Thurmond quavered. "They shine just like the ghost horse!"

Nancy switched on the light. Before them stood Chief, a large rubber ball clutched in his jaws.

Smiling at the flabbergasted onlookers, Nancy said, "Do you see how the phantom trick was worked?"

"I do," George said promptly. "Phosphorescent paint on the dog's teeth."

"Where are the specks now?" Mrs Thurmond asked as Chief dropped the ball.

"They don't show when the lights are on. At the time Chief disappeared—after he chased the phantom horse—the spots were on his teeth," Nancy explained. "I thought perhaps he had bitten the ghost, but when I examined him in daylight, of course I found no evidence."

"The gang must have washed him," remarked Bess.

"But they never thought of his teeth," Nancy said, "and fragments of the paint remained."

"How did you get on to the idea?" Aunt Bet asked.

Nancy reminded the others of her suspicion that Chief had been muzzled and taken away because the gang feared there was a clue to the apparition on him.

"I learned in chemistry class that phosphorescent paint glows in the dark after it first has been exposed to light," she went on. "I remembered that each time I'd seen the phantom horse there had been a light in the spring house just before. I put two and two together and decided that the apparition was a real horse. He was covered with a soft thin material which had been coated with phosphorescent paint and exposed to light in the spring house by one of the gang members."

Mrs Thurmond drew a deep breath and turned to Nancy. "You're a downright marvel, that's what you are, young lady!"

Nancy blushed. "You'll stay now, won't you?" And the others all added their pleas.

" 'Course I will," Mrs Thurmond declared stoutly. "You just show me the varmint that's been doing this no-good trick and I'll give him a piece o' my mind!"

Before going to bed, Nancy told Aunt Bet and Uncle Ed of her plan for the following day. The rancher assured her he would co-operate. At breakfast the girls talked lightheartedly of their all-day horseback ride.

"Where you gals fixin' to go?" Shorty asked.

"We'll start up Shadow Mountain," Nancy replied vaguely. "After that, we'll see."

Mr Rawley broke in to appoint Tex and Bud as his helpers on the "treasure" expedition.

When the meal was over, Nancy took Dave aside and told him that if she and the other girls found Valentine's hoard, they would light a fire on the lookout rock.

"Good," he replied. "Then I'll drive down the valley in the truck and climb up to the cliff houses by the front steps to help you bring the treasure back to the ranch."

Half an hour later Uncle Ed, Tex, and Bud saddled up for their trip. Shorty hung around, eager to help as two pack horses were led out. One was loaded with digging tools and other supplies.

"What's the second animal for?" asked Sanders, who had been told the secret.

The ranch owner grinned. "For the treasure."

The trio headed down the valley away from Tumbleweed. Shorty watched them for a minute, then hurried into the woods behind the ranch house. Strolling towards the stable, Nancy suspected that Bursey and Diamond were hiding among the trees, waiting to see which way the "treasure" party had gone.

In the tack room, Dave helped Nancy pack small digging tools into a saddlebag and wrap a spade in a blanket. The cowboy then saddled the girls' horses and slung the gear aboard two of them. Mrs Thurmond brought lunches which Dave added to a pack as Nancy called to her companions that everything was ready.

Before they mounted, Nancy suggested that they cross the big meadow. "We'll ride up Shadow Mountain from there."

"But it's in the opposite direction from the cliff dwellings," Alice whispered.

"That's the idea," Nancy replied. "Just in case Shorty suspects a trick and decides to follow us."

Dave pulled out a stub of pencil and drew a map for Nancy on the back of an envelope. It showed a trail going east across the mountain to the cliff dwellings.

Twenty minutes later the girls were heading up Shadow Mountain. As they jogged along the trail, Nancy studied the map and noted that Dave's route began not far from the cabin.

"We can go there first," she said. "If the gang is off on a wild-goose chase, now would be a good time to search for their hiding place."

Though the girls were eager to go on with their real purpose, they spent the morning wandering over various trails. "If anyone is following us, I hope he'll think we're just out for pleasure and give up the chase," Nancy remarked.

In early afternoon they stopped beside a stream to eat their lunch, then rode straight for the cabin. After half an hour, however, they were brought up short by huge boulders on the path.

"A rockfall!" George exclaimed. "We'll have to detour."

The riders backtracked, then crossed a steep stony slope, so treacherous that they were forced to dismount and lead their horses slowly. Finally, they reached clear trail again. It was mid-afternoon when Alice cried out, "There's the cabin! I see the roof."

The foursome rode up the slope and hitched their horses to pegs in the ground. Cautiously they made their way towards the cabin. The door was open and no one was inside.

Nancy led the way behind the cabin and noticed again how close the back window was to the brush screen and rock wall.

"What a funny place to put a window!" Bess remarked.

"Yes. That's one of the reasons I feel sure a hiding place is back here somewhere," Nancy replied. "I think the window was used as an escape exit from the cabin."

The girls examined the close-growing chaparral. A

few feet to the side of the window, George discovered a break in the thorny brush.

Nancy slipped into it, and one by one the girls struggled through and entered a narrow cleft in the rock wall.

A few yards inside the opening Nancy pointed out horseshoe, paw, and shoe prints. "Let's follow the prints," she suggested. "I have a hunch this path might lead to Valentine's hideout."

The girls hurried to their mounts, and soon were riding through the narrow pass with only a strip of blue sky visible above them.

After a while even that was blotted out by an overhang. The path grew gloomy and wound sharply round jagged outcrops.

By the time the riders saw daylight again, the sun was low in the sky. They rode up a gentle slope and found themselves on a high plateau. Some distance ahead was a long, straight rocky parapet about twelve feet high.

Nancy reined up sharply. "Look!" she cried out. Built against the wall was a three-sided stone enclosure with an old wooden gate. Inside pranced a handsome black stallion.

"The phantom horse!" Nancy exclaimed.

As the four riders approached, the animal whinnied and reared, backing towards a crude lean-to stable.

"Maybe the trick trappings are in there," George said.

Nancy dismounted quickly, opened the wooden gate, and slipped into the enclosure. The black steed whinnied nervously and shied away, but Nancy talked soothingly to him as she walked forward.

There was a pile of hay in a corner of the stable. Nancy felt under it. In a few moments her fingers encountered something soft and she pulled out a bundle of white material. She carried it outside and closed the gate behind her.

"The phantom costume!" Bess exclaimed as Nancy shook out the filmy cloth.

"It's thin silk material used for theatrical effects," Nancy told the girls. She tucked the cloth into her saddlebag.

"This stable looks old," Bess remarked. "I don't think the gang built it."

"You're right!" Alice exclaimed, and pointed to a barely discernible heart scratched on the gate.

"Then Valentine's hideout must be near here," Nancy said.

As the girls looked round, Nancy noticed a huge rock jutting from the far end of the parapet. With a thrill of excitement she recognized the lookout point. "We're on top of the cliff houses!" she exclaimed. "Let's get the wood ready for the fire, then start searching for the treasure."

Beyond the lookout rock the girls could see a grove of trees. They rode over and tethered their horses. The wind moaned through the fir trees and Nancy shivered. She took her sweater from the saddle horn and threw it over her shoulders. It was nearly dusk, so the girls hung torches on their belts.

Then they collected wood for the signal fire and carried it to the lookout rock just as the sun set. Nancy was the last to make her way off the rock. To one side of it was a short flight of worn steps going down to the top row of cliff houses.

Nancy was about to lead the descent when they heard the howl of a coyote. She stopped short.

"What's the matter?" asked Alice.

"Sh—listen!" Everyone froze. "I hope that's a real coyote," said Nancy.

Bess gasped. "You mean Shorty—"

"If the gang has discovered our ruse, they may have backtracked and traced us here," George said.

Nancy nodded. "We'd better not turn our lights on."

Hugging the parapet, the girls went down the steps to the narrow walk which ran in front of the houses. To their left was a sheer drop.

For a moment they stood still, breathless at the height and the silence. Suddenly there came a *thump* from the first room.

Bess grabbed George's arm and Alice gasped. Quietly Nancy stepped to the open doorway and peered into the gloom.

A man was lying on the floor!

19

The Cliff's Secret

"HELP!" called a feeble voice as Nancy shone her torch into the dim room.

"Daddy!" cried Alice and brushed past Nancy. She threw herself beside a thin grey-haired man who was bound hand and foot.

"Uncle Ross!" exclaimed Bess and George.

The older girls swiftly untied his bonds. Crying for joy, Alice helped her father sit up and the two embraced.

After introductions, Mr Regor explained that he had made the thumping noise by kicking his heels. "My throat was so parched I couldn't yell out to you."

Then Alice's father told his story. "I've been a prisoner in the cabin for six months—ever since they kidnapped me at the time of the bank robbery. But this morning the gang intended to go after the Rawley treasure party, so they moved me here, where they thought I wouldn't be discovered."

"Why did you go to the bank the night of the robbery, Daddy?" Alice asked.

"To get some important papers I had left there. I was working at home and needed them." He said he had interrupted the robbery, and the gang took him along to keep him from identifying them.

"They're Westerners," he went on, "and have used

this cabin hideout before. The idea was to stay here for a cooling-off period."

"How many are in the gang?" Nancy asked.

"Three. At first Shorty and Sid Brice stayed in the cabin with me while Al Diamond lived in Tumbleweed and brought us supplies."

"Who's Sid Brice, Uncle Ross?" Bess asked.

"The grey-haired fellow who looks like me."

"He calls himself Bursey," Nancy told him.

"I know," said Mr Regor. "One day Al Diamond came to the cabin all excited. He'd talked to an Indian girl named Mary Deer and learned all about Valentine's treasure. So Diamond decided that the gang should go after it and sent Shorty to get a job on the ranch. He was supposed to spread the phantom horse story and drive the Rawleys off."

Nancy looked troubled. "Mr Regor, what happened to the bank loot?"

"It was hidden in the cabin until Shorty reported that you girls had spotted the place.

"The next day Diamond and Brice moved the money to the ghost town and made me go along. They had just finished hiding the loot in the old hotel when we heard your horses approaching. Brice hustled me down the hill. All I could do was drop one of my crayons and hope somebody would find it."

"Oh, we did, Daddy!" exclaimed Alice.

Mr Regor said Diamond had remained in the ghost town to spy on the girls. "Later he told us he had caused a rockslide."

Nancy mentioned finding the coffee cups on the table in the cabin.

"Yes. We heard your horses clattering up the slope,

so Brice forced me out through the window at the back and into the little rocky passage. He had the dog on a rope and made him go too. But later he broke loose."

"We found one of your pictures on the table, Uncle Ross," said George.

The man smiled. "I've been drawing pictures to keep myself busy. Brice has been selling them and keeping the money for himself," he added.

"Those terrible men! Have they mistreated you, Daddy?"

The bank president said he had not been hurt, but had been underfed and was weak. "I once heard Brice say there was time enough to get rid of me when they left Shadow Mountain."

While Alice told her father all that had happened so far, Nancy, Bess, and George flashed their lights about Mr Regor's prison.

The floor was littered with pieces of broken pottery and rock. Beside the door Nancy noticed a flat-topped boulder. "The Indians probably used it for a table, or a seat," she thought. Nearby was a large rectangular chunk of stone.

The three girls switched off their lights and stepped outside. With Nancy in the lead, the three friends walked close to the wall of the cliff dwellings. They searched one apartment after another for the treasure, but always found the same thing: shards and crumbled rocks.

As the girls emerged from one of the middle rooms, Nancy noticed a crude wooden ladder resting against the wall and leading to the roof.

"It's just an old ladder—probably put there by the cliff dwellers," said Bess.

Nancy did not agree. "There are nails in this. Perhaps Valentine brought it here. I'd like to climb up."

"Let's finish searching the rooms," George said.

"Okay."

As they neared the end of the row, the young detective exclaimed, "Look!" The last doorway was neatly blocked with an enormous stone.

"Valentine's hideout!" exclaimed George. "He must have put that rock there to keep intruders out!"

"But how did he get in?" Bess asked, puzzled. "The stone's too big to be moved much on this little ledge."

"I know!" exclaimed Nancy. "Come on!" She hastened back to the ladder. Swiftly she attached her torch to her belt and slipped her arms into her sweater.

By the time Bess and George caught up to Nancy, she had begun to climb. Breathlessly they watched her as she cautiously tested each rung. One splintered before she finally reached the roof.

"Nancy, be careful!" Bess cried fearfully.

Shading the beam of her torch, Nancy moved towards the end chamber and found a column of ancient footholds to the plateau above.

"Probably there's another set like them on the other side," she reasoned. "The ladder was Valentine's extra escape route."

Playing the torchlight over the surface, Nancy walked a dozen steps towards the end of the roof. Suddenly she spotted a large hole.

Shining her light into it, Nancy saw a pile of broken rock directly below. She gripped the sides of the opening and lowered herself into the chamber.

"O-oo, it's musty in here!"

In one corner lay a mouldering blanket and saddle.

Nearby was a pick-axe. On the wall above these Nancy found an indistinct carved letter. She brushed away the dust.

V—for Valentine!

Nancy's pulse pounded with joy and excitement.

But where was the treasure? "It can't be buried," she thought. "The floor is solid stone."

When Nancy lifted the blanket, it fell into shreds at her touch. There was nothing beneath it. Her eyes fell upon a large pottery vase in the corner. The vessel was nearly three feet high and had a wide mouth. Nancy beamed her light into it.

Standing on end and level with the top of the vase was a metal box!

"This might be it!" Nancy exulted. She put down her torch, reached in, and lifted out the heavy box. It slipped from her grasp and hit the floor, jolting off a rusted padlock.

Nancy pulled open the lid. Before her lay hundreds of small shining gold hearts!

"Oh!"

Beneath the layer of gold pieces lay stacks of United States bank notes and a chamois leather bag. It contained an assortment of precious jewels!

"It can't be real!" Nancy said aloud. "I'm dreaming!"

But Nancy's mind clicked back to reality. "I can't get this chest back through the ceiling, that's for sure." She eyed the pick-axe. "Maybe I can pry the rock away from the door."

Nancy worked the point of the pick-axe beneath the rock. She pulled hard. The slab moved a trifle! She tried again. This time the rock moved about a foot.

Nancy pushed the treasure box through the opening, turned off her torch, and squeezed outside.

"George! Bess!" The girls came running and Nancy told of her find. "Take the treasure back to Alice and Mr Regor," she directed. "I'll light the signal fire."

Cautiously Nancy crawled out on to the jutting rock and took a packet of matches from her pocket. She struck one, shielding it from the wind, and held it to the kindling.

As the smoke rose, a gruff voice behind her suddenly barked, "Put out that fire!"

· 20 ·

Daring Tactics

THE voice was Al Diamond's. Nancy was trapped on the jutting rock, far above the valley!

"Stamp out that blaze!" the man repeated sharply, "or I'll knock you off there!"

"All right!" Nancy's brain was in a whirl. She delayed until Diamond bellowed again, then she kicked the pile of smouldering wood from the rock. It burst into a shower of sparks and flame on the way down.

Diamond snarled, "Come here!" When Nancy made her way back to the cliff, he said gloatingly:

"You think you're smart. As for those phoney treasure hunters, we cut out of that trap when I spotted the sheriff trailing us."

Nancy's spirits sank as Al continued to storm. "You've made it too hot for us here, and you'll pay for it."

He said the gang was on its way to the ghost town to pick up the bank loot when they stopped at the cabin. Shorty found fresh horse tracks and guessed the girls had a line on the treasure.

"He saw you gathering wood and gave us his coyote signal."

Nancy's captor bragged that he and his partners had

hurried to the top of the steps and watched from above. Seeing the girls emerging from Regor's prison, the three men had sneaked down into one of the cliff-dwelling rooms to spy on them.

"Finally we saw you hurry by, and then your friends showed up, carrying something heavy. I said to myself, 'There goes the treasure. How nice to have Nancy Drew do all the work for us!'"

"You didn't harm Bess and George!" Nancy said hotly.

"Oh no," came the sarcastic reply. "My boys let 'em get to Regor's prison, then they closed in."

Nancy fumbled for her torch and switched it on.

"Turn that off! I don't want anybody getting nosey. Hurry up! Get going!"

Nancy hoped desperately that Dave had seen the signal fire. In order to give him time to make the treacherous ascent, Nancy hugged the wall and moved as slowly as possible.

"Step on it!" Diamond barked. Finally he pushed her into the prison room. In one corner she saw the red glow of a torch shaded by a cloth, and near it the dark figures of two men. But she could see nothing else in the room.

"We're okay, Nancy," came George's voice. "They made us sit on the floor."

"And smashed our torches," said Bess.

Diamond spoke up sharply. "Shorty, where's that treasure?"

"Can't see it, Boss. You told me to keep the light covered."

Diamond fumbled about before giving an exclamation of disgust. "Regor, are you hiding it?"

"Leave my father alone!" Alice cried out. "He doesn't have anything."

Instantly Nancy's foot reached for the large chunk of stone she had seen near the door. Quickly she shrugged her sweater from her shoulders and it dropped over the stone.

"All right, Mr Diamond. Here it is!"

As she spoke, Nancy stooped and gathered the rock into her sweater.

"I'll take it!"

"No, you won't!" With a mighty lunge Nancy hurled the stone through the door and over the side of the cliff. Seconds later it crashed on the rocks below.

For a moment there was a stunned silence. Then Diamond exploded. "You've played your last trick on me, Nancy Drew. Brice! Shorty! Tie 'em up!"

Nancy sat on the stone bench beside the door and waited coolly while Shorty lashed her ankles together.

Diamond said, "Brice, you and I'll go down to the valley and find the treasure. Shorty, guard these girls till you get my signal."

At this Nancy chuckled. "Poor Shorty! By the time you reach the valley, your pals and the treasure will be gone."

The cowboy stopped his tying and turned to Diamond. "Let Brice stay. I'm through stickin' my neck out!"

"Yes," Nancy declared, "suspicion was on you from the beginning. You wrecked the pump and cut the telephone wire."

"All right," Shorty said resentfully. "And I put the generator out of action and pulled the nettle trick."

"Shut up!" Diamond ordered.

George spoke up. "They kept you busy, Shorty.

After you imitated poor Chief you found the clue in Nancy's watch and later stole the green liniment bottle."

Out of the darkness came Bess's voice. "Who ransacked our room?"

"Brice," replied Shorty, "and that's about all he did!"

"What do you mean?" Brice interrupted. "I cut the fences and knocked down the windmill!"

"Is that so!" Diamond spluttered angrily. "Without my brains, you'd both be nowhere!"

Now the men's voices shrilled in anger as each claimed importance for his part in the conspiracy.

Diamond's voice rose with fury. "Listen," he raged, "I got the idea for the phantom horse. I bought the silk and paint and trained the stallion to come to my whistle."

"We helped you!" Shorty retorted. He reminded Diamond that he and Brice had put the trappings on the stallion for the phantom performance.

Ross Regor cut in. "You almost caught them at it one night, Nancy. Scared them so badly they called off the phantom. I heard Brice say he had to slip from the spring house into the cellar through the secret opening."

"Quit wasting time," Diamond shrieked. "We've got to clear out of here!"

"Now take it easy, Diamond," Shorty said with a ring of authority. "It's me and Brice agin you. We'll go for the treasure. You stay here."

Diamond fumed. "Okay. But don't try any funny business. And come right back."

Without a word, the other two men went out of the door, taking the light with them. The captives heard Diamond make his way through the darkness to the back of the chamber, then heard the creak of a hinge.

A soft laugh came from the gang leader. "In case you're wondering, I'm opening a wooden box where we keep dynamite and fuses."

Gasps came from the prisoners. "You can't do that!" George cried out.

"I'm forced to. Ross Regor knows too much, and I can't afford to let him go. Too bad, Nancy Drew, that you butted into my affairs."

"I'll stay," Mr Regor cried out. "But don't harm these girls!"

"No! And as soon as I light the fuse, I'll get out of here."

Crack! A match flared in Diamond's hand.

"Wait!" Nancy exclaimed. "You'll blow up the treasure!"

The match hovered in mid-air. "What?"

"That was just a big stone I threw over the cliff," Nancy admitted.

She turned on her torch and swept it about the room, making certain the beam hit the entrance several times. Someone just might notice it.

"Here! Give me that!" Diamond snatched the light. "Now where's the thing you girls carried?"

"Here," said Bess, "we're sitting on it."

Diamond pushed her and George aside and flipped open the chest. "Well I never!" He grabbed a handful of the gold hearts and let them run through his fingers. Then he closed the lid and began to carry the box towards the entrance.

Just then the rattle of falling stones came from below. Flushed with success, Diamond called out, "Shorty! Brice! I have the treasure! Fellows, we're rich!"

Voices! Then a light flashed into the room.

"Hold it, Diamond!"

"*Dave!*" Nancy cried out.

Diamond made a break for freedom, but George put out her foot and the criminal fell into the strong arms of Sheriff Curtis. Handcuffs clicked shut.

The girls and Mr Regor gave shouts of joy at the sight of Dave, the sheriff, his deputy, and Mr Rawley. As the captives were untied, Ross Regor told how cleverly Nancy had played for time.

Dave smiled. "She's the smartest little tenderfoot I ever saw." Then he related how the decoys and the sheriff's party had lost the gang and gone back to Shadow Ranch.

"When we saw the fire falling, I figured something like this had happened."

Mr Rawley said, "We didn't want to give ourselves away, so we drove up the valley with our lights off."

Dave added that Brice and Shorty had been caught on the way down. "But where's the treasure?"

"Here." George grinned.

Half an hour later, the party reached the valley floor just as the moon rose. Dave put Valentine's fortune in the estate car while Nancy gave Sheriff Curtis a brief report. It was agreed that he would recover the stolen bank money from the ghost-town hotel in the morning and the cowboys were to bring in the girls' horses and the "phantom". The sullen prisoners were driven off in the sheriff's car.

As Dave headed the car down the valley, he said he thought Nancy should have a share of the treasure. "I know the gold must be turned over to the state," Dave added. "But the jewels and bank notes should be worth a good sum. Nancy, since you found them, I feel a share rightfully belongs to you."

The young detective smiled, then graciously but firmly declined to accept any part of the find. "It was fun," she said.

The grateful cowboy grinned. "My brother and sister sure will be excited by the news."

A little later they turned into the gate. The ranch, bathed in silvery moonlight, looked peaceful.

Alice squeezed her father's hand. "Everything has turned out happily!"

"Thanks to Nancy Drew." Mr Regor smiled.

"What are you going to do now, Nancy, without a mystery to solve?" Bess teased.

Her friend smiled. "Work on the sweater I'm knitting for Ned." She did not know then that soon she would become involved in the thrilling *Mystery of the 99 Steps*.

But George knew that Nancy and mystery were never far apart. She gave a sigh of mock sadness. "Poor Ned! I hope he doesn't need that sweater in the near future!"

Armada now publish an exciting new mystery series—

The Hardy Boys Adventure Stories

by Franklin W. Dixon

The escapades of Frank and Joe Hardy, sons of a famous detective, and their staunch friend, Chet Morton, lead to breathtaking dangers and adventures. If you can't resist a gripping plot, daring heroes, death-dealing villains, hair's-breadth escapes and plenty of action, the Hardy Boys are for you!

These are the first four thrilling stories—

The Mystery of the Aztec Warrior

The Arctic Patrol Mystery

The Haunted Fort

The Mystery of the Whale Tattoo

And the next six, to be published soon, will be:

The Mystery of the Desert Giant

The Mystery of the Melted Coins

The Mystery of the Spiral Bridge

The Clue of the Screeching Owl

While the Clock Ticked

The Twisted Claw

Watch out for more Hardy Boys adventures.

Armada

Armada books are chosen by children all over the world. They're designed to fit your pocket, and your pocket money too – why not build up your own Armada library? There are hundreds of exciting titles and favourite series to collect, and their bright spines look marvellous on any bookshelf. Armada have something for everyone:

Books by popular authors like **Enid Blyton – Malcolm Saville – Elinor Brent-Dyer – Alfred Hitchcock,** etc.

The best mysteries and most exciting adventure stories.

Favourite characters like **Jennings – William – Nancy Drew – The Hardy Boys – Biggles – The Three Investigators – The Lone Piners –** and many, many more.

Pony books by the Pullein-Thompson sisters, Mary Gervaise and Judith Berrisford.

A wonderful collection of famous children's stories.

Ghost books to make your hair stand on end!

A terrific collection of **quiz, puzzle and fun books** to entertain you for hours.

These are just a few of the good things Armada has in store for you.

If you'd like a complete up-to-date list of Armada books, send a stamped, addressed envelope to:

> Armada Books,
> 14 St James's Place,
> London SW1.